CROSSCUT

Published by Thomas & Mercer
P.O. Box 400818
Las Vegas, NV 89140

ISBN-13: 9781612183114
ISBN-10: 1612183115

CROSSCUT
a nicholas colt thriller

JUDE HARDIN

THOMAS & MERCER

CHAPTER ONE

Anyone who says they're not afraid of death has probably never stared it straight in the eye. They've probably never had a knife held to their throat, or the barrel of a revolver pressed against their forehead. They've probably never been pinned against the bulkhead of a plummeting airplane.

Those were my thoughts as I headed south on Florida State Road 21, toward a little town called Melrose and a little seafood restaurant called Blue Water Bay.

On the radio, some author I'd never heard of promoted some book she wrote about coping with mortality. She claimed to be completely unafraid of death herself. When the time came, she said, she would embrace it with passion.

I wondered how passionate she would be if a hungry tiger entered the studio and started gnawing on her face.

I switched off the radio. Embrace it with passion, my ass. Rule #10 in Nicholas Colt's *Philosophy of Life*: Do not go gentle into that good night.

I stole rule #10 from a poet named Dylan Thomas.

It was Fat Tuesday, *Mardi Gras*, and I was meeting an old friend named Donna Wahl—*Prescott* now, I reminded myself—for cocktails and dinner. Donna had something important she wanted to talk to me about.

I still had several miles to go when my cell phone trilled.

I picked up. "This is Nicholas Colt."

"Hey, Daddy."

It was Brittney, my adopted daughter. She had been with my wife, Juliet, and me for nearly three years, and my heart still melted every time she called me Daddy.

"Hi, sweetheart," I said. "How was school?"

"School sucks. I can't wait to be done with it and start college in the fall."

You can never convince a seventeen-year-old how great it is to be seventeen. I skipped the lecture and said, "You're almost done. Hey, I thought you had that thing at the skating rink tonight."

"That's why I called. I have a flat tire."

"Where are you?"

"On Paradise. A guy helped me push the car into Walmart's parking lot."

"I'm about thirty miles the other direction. Did you call the auto club?"

"No."

"They'll change the tire for you. But listen, I don't want you driving around on that little emergency spare. Once they change it, go straight home. We'll get your tire fixed tomorrow."

Silence.

"Brit?"

"OK," she said, noticeably irritated at the thought of being without transportation for an entire evening.

"I'll be home around nine or nine thirty," I said. "See you then."

"Bye."

We disconnected. I made a mental note to call her in an hour to make sure she arrived home safely.

I steered into the parking lot of Blue Water Bay. I parked and walked inside, my hands fisted in the pockets of my leather jacket. Donna was waiting at the bar. She stood and greeted me with a hug.

"Cold as hell out there," I said.

"Well, let's see what we can do about getting you warmed up."

I sat beside her and ordered an Old Fitz on the rocks. I took a sip, felt a trail of fire from the tip of my tongue to the deepest part of my stomach.

"Better?" she asked.

"Yeah. Can I get you another one of those?" I gestured toward her martini glass.

"Actually, I'm ready for dinner if you are."

"OK."

We settled up at the bar and walked to the dining room entrance where a hostess led us to our table. Donna was three years younger than me, but at forty-five she still looked great in tight black pants and a cranberry sweater. Her hair was shoulder length and expensively dyed, and she might have gotten a nose job at some point. We sat and opened our menus.

"I heard you got married," Donna said.

"I did. After I lost Susan, I said never again. But I guess the old saying is true."

"Who is she?"

"Her name's Juliet. She's from the Philippines. She's a nurse."

I pulled my wallet out and showed Donna my family portrait. She asked about Brittney and I told her the story.

"How's the writing going?" I said. Donna wrote true crime books and magazine stories.

"Tough to sell anything right now. I'm thinking about getting a new agent."

A muscular waiter with a military buzz cut and fake diamond earrings introduced himself as Brian and asked if he could get us anything to drink. We ordered another round and some crab nachos. I remembered they were Donna's favorite.

She closed her menu and took a sip from her water glass. "I know you're probably wondering why I wanted you to meet me here. It's about my brother, Derek. He's been missing for over fourteen months."

"Missing from where?"

"He's a police officer in a little town in Tennessee called Black Creek. He went on a call a year ago Thanksgiving, a domestic disturbance, and then just disappeared. They found his car parked at the curb outside the address he was called to, but no Derek. He just vanished. Without a trace, as they say."

"Any signs of foul play?"

"Plenty. There were two bodies in the dining room, the elderly woman who lived in the house and her widowed daughter-in-law. The elderly woman's husband and their twenty-seven-year-old grandson are also missing. They were all recently declared legally dead, but I can't accept that. I know in my heart Derek is still alive."

"Any suspects in the murder case?"

"Not really, although the police found some DNA at the scene that didn't belong to Derek or any of the family there. The couple didn't have any money to speak of, no big insurance policies. I was just wondering—"

"If I would go up there and take a look around?"

"Yes. It would mean a lot to me. Derek is my only living relative, and I—"

She broke then. She pulled a miniature package of tissues from her purse, pinched a few from the slit in the plastic wrapper, and used them to dab the tears from her eyes.

Brian arrived with our drinks and appetizer and took our dinner order. By the time he walked away, Donna seemed to have regained her composure.

"I'm sorry," she said.

"No need to be. Listen, Donna, I would love to help you out, but I'm not doing the private eye thing anymore. I don't even have a license. I let it go inactive."

"So what are you doing now?"

"I put a little band together. We have a house gig at a club in Jacksonville."

She was still clutching her tissue, which was now twisted and resembled a short and skinny length of rope. She pulled the speared olives from her drink and downed the remaining vodka in a single gulp.

"Good for you," she said.

Brian delivered our food. Donna and I relaxed and ate and drank and talked about some of the good times we'd had together a long time ago. The blackened fish was as delicious as any I'd ever eaten. I was about to take my last bite when the phone in my pocket vibrated.

The caller ID said Juliet. She was calling from her cell phone, but I knew she was still at work. I asked Donna to please excuse me.

"Hey, babe," I said.

"Nicholas, have you heard from Brittney?"

"I talked to her a while ago. She had a flat tire on Paradise, and I told her to call the auto club. She should be home by now. I was fixing to call and check up on her."

"A flat? Oh, great. I've left voice mail, and I've texted, but she's not getting back to me. I know she was supposed to go skating tonight, but I'm starting to get worried. It's not like her to not answer her phone."

"I told her to go straight home after they changed the tire. That Camry has one of those little bicycle tires for a spare, and I didn't want her out driving around on it. I'm sure she's all right. Maybe she fell asleep. I'm leaving Melrose in a few minutes and heading home. I'll give you a call when I get there."

"Please do. How's your date going?"

"I'll tell you later. Love you."

"Love you too. Bye."

I tried Brittney's number, got voice mail. I put the phone back in my pocket.

Brian asked if we wanted dessert, but neither of us did. He brought the check, and Donna insisted on paying. I left some cash on the table for a tip.

I walked Donna to her car. My hair was long enough to cover my ears and I had a full beard, but the February wind still chilled me to the marrow. It wasn't supposed to be this cold in Florida.

"I know a guy in Nashville who might be able to help you," I said. "Pete Strong. I met him at a convention a few years ago. Strong Investigations. Google it. You'll find contact info on his website. Just tell him Nicholas Colt sent you."

"I'll do that. Thank you. God, it's so horrible not knowing. I guess I'm expecting the worst, but I need some sort of closure. And those people who were murdered, just ghastly. Whoever did it mutilated them, you know. Carved crosses on them. I can't imagine—"

"Wait," I said. "What was that about crosses?"

"One of Derek's fellow officers emailed me some pictures of the women who were murdered. From the autopsies. Oh, Nicholas, it was horrible. Both of them had what looked like slanted crucifixes carved into their foreheads…"

Donna kept talking, but my mind had drifted elsewhere.

Slanted crucifixes.

That changed everything.

CHAPTER TWO

Soon after we got married, Juliet and I bought a nice three-bedroom ranch in a nice subdivision. All the residents have nice yards and nice automobiles, and all the nice little doggies are kept on leashes studded with rhinestones. Many of the thirtysomethings take nice runs every morning, hoping to extend their nice little lives to a ripe old age. They have ski boats and iPhones and televisions bigger than their dining room tables. Everything is just really nice.

I hate it.

I used to live in a 1964 Airstream Safari travel trailer. I still have it, and it's still parked on lot 27 at Joe's Fish Camp. Joe is my best friend. He gives me a good rate. Sometimes I go out there by myself for a day or two, just to get away from all the niceness.

Our house is on the end of a cul-de-sac, and before I reached the driveway I could see Brittney's car was not there. I drove back out of the subdivision and headed north on Paradise. Fifteen minutes later I steered into Walmart, thinking she might still be there waiting for her tire to be changed. She was not.

I continued north for a few more miles and hung a left into the parking lot of the skating rink. One of Brittney's friends from school belonged to a roller derby team, and Brittney had planned to go watch her skate and maybe get involved in the sport herself. That was before the flat tire.

I cruised to the back of the building and saw Brittney's Camry parked off in a corner. The windows were fogged. I parked, killed the engine, walked to the Camry, knocked on the driver's side window. The radio was playing so I knew someone was in there. I knocked again, tried the handle but it was locked.

"Open the goddamn door," I said.

Brittney wiped a peephole from the backseat and peered through with one eye. The locks clicked. She opened the door and stepped out. It was probably about thirty degrees outside, and there were beads of sweat on her forehead. The boy in the backseat sat slouched with his arms folded over his chest. He should have been more nervous than he looked, because I was about to yank him out of the car and modify his face in a very uncomplimentary fashion.

"You got about three seconds to disappear, partner," I said.

"This is Justin," Brittney said. "I was going to give him a ride home."

"Justin needs to start walking, while he's still able."

"He lives up past a Hundred and Third Street. You can't make him walk home in this weather. Come on, Dad. Be reasonable."

"Brittney, do you have any idea how pissed I am right now? Do you?"

"It's all right, Brit," Justin said. He exited the other side of the car and started walking toward the supermarket next door. "I'll call a cab." He huffed away with his hands buried deep in the pockets of his jeans. He was about six feet tall with bushy brown hair and the beginnings of an immature beard.

I turned my attention back to Brittney. "Why didn't you go home like I told you to?"

"I wanted to see Marla skate."

"From the backseat of your car?"

She looked at her shoes. "Daddy, it's cold. Can we just go home now?"

"Why didn't you answer your phone?"

"The battery died. Please, I'm freezing out here."

"All right. You go straight to the house. I'll be right behind you."

"You're not going to yell at me when we get there, are you?"

"Yes. I am."

"God." She raked that beautiful long blonde hair of hers back with her fingers, climbed into the Camry, and started the engine.

On the way home, I called Juliet to let her know everything was all right.

—◊◊◊—

I put on a black turtleneck, started a fire in the fireplace, and sat there in my leather recliner with a shot of Grand Marnier in a brandy snifter. I'd told Brittney that I wanted to talk to her when she got out of the shower. She came into the living room twenty minutes later wearing a pink terrycloth robe and a towel on her head. I had refilled my liquor glass by then.

Brittney pressed a wad of tissues against her right nostril. "You look like something out of a movie," she said. "Like some sort of weird lord of an English manor or something."

"Is your nose bleeding again?"

"I'm all right."

"How old was that guy?"

"Justin?"

"Yeah."

"I don't know."

"I think you do know. Tell me."

"He's twenty-one, OK? He's in college. A math major. He's a very nice guy."

"Are you having sex with him?"

"O. M. G. I cannot believe you just asked me that."

"Well, I'm pretty sure he wasn't tutoring you for a calculus test a while ago."

"Are we done? Because I'm really tired and I have to get up early."

"We're done. I'm going to let your mom talk to you about this. In the meantime, you're grounded."

"Grounded? What are you talking about? Dad, I'm almost eighteen."

"I don't care if you're almost eighty. As long as you're living under this roof, you will follow the rules. One of those rules is to do what I specifically tell you to do, and I specifically told you—"

"So what does grounded mean?"

"It means no car for the next two weeks."

"Two weeks? How am I supposed to get to school in the morning?"

"The same way you got there before you got your license."

"I am *not* riding the bus."

"That's a shame, because it's a really long walk."

"This is so not fair!" She rose abruptly and stalked away to her bedroom, slamming the door behind her.

I got up and put another log on the fire. I stood there for a few minutes, wondering if the punishment I'd imposed was too harsh. Brittney was a smart girl, but she had been through a lot before Juliet and I adopted her. Hell and back was an understatement.

She had lived on the streets for a while, and a religious cult called the Harvest Angels had abducted her. I saved her minutes before they would have burned her at the stake.

She suffered from post-traumatic stress disorder, and her judgment wasn't always up to snuff. Even for a seventeen-year-old. She was in counseling, and getting better, but I frequently had to remind myself that her thought processes weren't always what most people would consider normal. I had to keep an extra-close eye on her.

I decided two weeks without wheels was appropriate enough. Not only would it teach her a lesson, it would give Juliet a chance for some rare face time with her in the evenings.

I sat at my computer desk and logged onto the Internet. Donna had promised to forward the autopsy pictures she had gotten from the deputy in Tennessee. Sure enough, there was already a message from her in my inbox. I opened it and downloaded the photographs and the accompanying information.

A member of the Harvest Angels had murdered Brittney's sister, Leitha. A cross, tilted slightly to the right, had been carved into her forehead, same as the ones on the victims at the Lambs' residence.

I didn't want to go to Tennessee.

I didn't want to investigate these crimes.

I poured myself another drink and thought about it and fell asleep in front of the fire.

CHAPTER THREE

I drove Brittney to the bus stop the next morning so she wouldn't have to stand and wait in the cold. She gave me the silent treatment, not even bothering to say bye when she left my car to board the bus.

Along with everything else, I think she was embarrassed to be seen in my 1996 GMC Jimmy. Can't say I blame her. Faded silver paint, missing hubcaps, bubbled tint. It's not much to look at, but it's paid for and it gets me around. And the cargo space is great for hauling my guitars and amplifiers.

The bus disappeared into the fog, and I drove the Jimmy on back to the house. I was sitting at my computer with a third cup of coffee when Juliet got home from her shift at the hospital. She shuffled in wearily, hugged me from behind, and kissed my neck.

"You're up early," she said.

"I had to take Brittney to the bus stop. Did you know she's seeing someone who's twenty-one?"

"Twenty-one? No. Who is it?"

"Some guy named Justin. He's a math major in college, supposedly. I caught them making out in the back of her car. I told

Brittney you'd talk to her about it. In the meantime, she's grounded. No car for the next two weeks."

"I'll talk to her. When you say making out—"

"They still had all their clothes on. The thing is, I told Brittney to go straight home after her tire was changed. That's mostly why she's in trouble."

I rubbed my eyes, swallowed a mouthful of coffee. It had gotten lukewarm and tasted like singed hair.

"Are you OK?" Juliet asked. "You look as tired as I feel."

"Didn't sleep worth a shit last night."

"How come?"

"I'm going to show you something, but I have to warn you it's pretty gruesome."

She laughed. "It can't be any more gruesome than what I encounter at work every night."

"Believe me, it is."

I clicked on the first image from the file Donna had sent me.

"My God, Nicholas, that's horrible. Who is that?"

"This is Edna Lamb. Actually, this is Edna Lamb's torso. She was four days shy of her eighty-fourth birthday when she and her daughter-in-law were butchered. Here's her face. See anything significant?"

"It looks like a crucifix."

"Bingo. Leitha had the exact same mark in the exact same place."

"But the man who killed Leitha is dead."

"Very."

Juliet sipped from my cup as I scrolled through the entire set of autopsy photos. Her stomach for gore—and bad coffee—was stronger than I'd imagined.

"I'm trying to understand what happened here," she said. "Is this what they call a copycat?"

"Maybe. Or maybe it's the Harvest Angels again."

Just saying the words out loud made me sick to my stomach. The Harvest Angels were the militant branch of a white supremacist cult called the Chain of Light. I was instrumental in shutting them down in Florida three years ago. During the investigation, I found out they were responsible for the plane crash that killed my first wife and our baby daughter and all the members of my band. I'd helped shut them down in Florida, but rumor had it there were other cells in other places.

"I thought all those people were in jail now," Juliet said.

"The local ones are. These murders took place in Tennessee."

"So what does any of this have to do with you?"

I told her about Donna Wahl's missing brother, and about Donna wanting me to go up to Tennessee to investigate.

"I'm thinking about doing it," I said.

"But you're not a private investigator anymore. I don't want you to be a private investigator anymore."

"How can I just leave it alone? If it is the Harvest Angels—"

"So every time these neo-Nazi fuckwads kill someone, you're going to go hunt them down? That's crazy, Nicholas."

"Not every time. Just this time."

"What about the band?"

"That's no problem. I know plenty of guys who would jump at the chance to sub for us."

"Do you still love her?"

"Who?"

"Donna."

"Jules, that was a long time ago. Come here." I put my arm around her waist and gently pulled her toward me, guiding her to sit on my lap. "You're the only one I love. And that's forever."

We kissed, long and deep, and then Juliet rested her head on my shoulder. "I still don't want you to go."

"It'll only be for a few days."

"Promise?"

"Promise."

She kissed my ear, making soft, warm circles with her tongue. "I should go to bed now," she whispered. "Want to come tuck me in?"

"I'd love to."

—m—

I drove Brittney's Camry to the tire store and had them patch her tire and change the oil. I had decided to use it for my trip to Tennessee. With it gone, Brittney wouldn't be as tempted to fudge on her punishment. She could always take my Jimmy for a spin, but I doubted she would.

I stopped at the grocery store and bought some steaks and a bag of charcoal briquettes for the grill. I wanted us to have a nice family dinner together before I left. Then I spent the rest of the morning and early afternoon doing some research on the computer and making some phone calls. I called Donna and told her I was going to take the job after all. We came to an agreement on a retainer and an hourly rate, and she said she would have the money wired to Mont Falcon. And I called Pete Strong, the private investigator in Nashville I'd told Donna about, and let him know I was coming up and would need some help.

"What kind of help?" he said.

"I'm going to need a temporary license, some credentials I can show people I interview, and so forth."

"When are you coming?"

"I should be up there by late tomorrow afternoon. I'll be staying at the motel in Mont Falcon."

"Cool," Pete said. "I'm going to be in the area tomorrow anyway, so I'll meet you there. Just give me a call when you get in. I'll bring the stuff you need."

"Thanks, man. I owe you one."

"You owe me ten, but who's counting?"

Pete and I disconnected, and I sat there for a while and wondered if I was doing the right thing.

Brittney sauntered in a little after two o'clock. Her backpack—which weighed approximately the same as a stack of bricks—slid off her shoulder and landed with a thud on the foyer floor. She stabbed at her phone with her thumbs, trying her best to ignore me as she made a beeline toward her bedroom.

"Still not talking to me?" I said.

She glanced up, her thumbs still working feverishly on the touch screen. "Huh?"

"Put the phone down and come over here. Please."

She finished the text she was working on, walked to my desk, plopped down on the carpet, and sat Indian-style. "What?"

"How was school?"

"We got our interims today. I got all As except English."

"What did you get in English?"

"I got a B. Because of stupid *Hamlet.*"

"Nothing wrong with a B. I'm very proud of you."

She started to get up. "Bs won't get me into the University of Florida. I have homework. I'll be in my room, OK?"

"Wait a minute. I wanted to tell you, I'm going to be leaving town for a few days."

"Why?"

"I have some business up in Tennessee."

"What kind of business?"

"I'm going to go visit an old friend. I'll only be gone for a few days."

"Isn't your band supposed to play?"

"Rick Moody and his crew are going to cover for us."

"Oh. OK."

"I'm taking your car."

Her jaw dropped and her eyes got big. "What? What am I supposed to drive? And don't even say that piece of —"

"Hey. That's enough. You're not supposed to drive anything, because you're grounded. Remember? And keep your voice down. Your mom's trying to sleep."

"You're impossible, Dad. You better not tear my car up."

She rose then and stomped to her bedroom and shut the door. At least she didn't slam it this time.

CHAPTER FOUR

I left home early the next morning. On the way to the interstate, I stopped by my camper on Lake Barkley to pick up my favorite carry weapon, a .38-caliber revolver I call Little Bill. When we got married, Juliet made it clear she didn't want a bunch of guns in the house, so I keep most of my collection locked in the Airstream. Most. There's a loaded .357 Magnum strapped to the bottom of our bed frame at home, a gun that could stop a moose. I coaxed Juliet to the firing range one day and taught her how to shoot it accurately, against the advice of some friends. The friends were joking. I think.

I drove up the gravel driveway to my campsite, killed the engine, and got out. The sandy-haired dog we call Bud trotted from behind my camper with a length of nylon rope clenched in his teeth. Bud has some Great Dane in him. He looks like a Labrador on steroids. Dylan Crawford, my friend Joe's son, likes to think Bud is his dog, but Bud belongs to nobody. I like that about him. He showed up at the lake one day a few years ago, mangy and half-starved. Joe took him to the vet and got him straightened out, and he's been the community pet ever since.

I played tug-of-war with him for a few minutes, and then gave him a vigorous back rub.

"I gotta go, Bud."

He dropped the rope and wagged his tail, obviously hoping I might let him tag along.

"Maybe next time," I said, scratching his ears. I opened the Airstream, got Little Bill and a box of .38 shells. There was a moldy loaf of bread on the table, so I grabbed it on my way out and tossed it into the rusty drum we use for burning trash. Bud looked at me as though I were insane. I gave him one last pat on the head, started the Camry, and pointed it toward Tennessee.

—✕—

I made it to Mont Falcon at around four in the afternoon. Less than a mile from the exit ramp there was a Piggly Wiggly, a Sunoco station, and a motel attached to a restaurant called Moe's Ribs. I parked and walked up to a swinging glass door that said LOBBY. Patchy remnants of snow dotted the landscape.

The clerk stood hunched over a computer keyboard at the counter. Midsixties, saggy wrinkled face, bright red hair showing gray at the roots. She glanced up at me through a pair of lenses that could have doubled for drink coasters. Her name tag said Beulah.

"Be right with you," she said.

There was a vending machine against the wall where you could buy forgotten necessities like toothbrushes and razors, along with miniature books of crossword puzzles and cheap decks of playing cards. Beside the vending machine, a beige steel rack held a bunch of brochures with information on local attractions. I picked up one about a fishing rodeo and dreamed of warmer days.

"Can I help you, sir?"

"I need a room, please."

"Just the one night?"

"I'll be here a few days."

"Would you like a king, or two queens?"

"A king is fine."

She did her thing on the keyboard. "Do you qualify for our senior citizen discount?"

She obviously didn't know I had a .38 holstered under my jacket.

—m—

I opened the door to what could have been any cheap motel room in any part of the country. Garish drapes and bedspread, a framed print of ducks flying over a pond, carpeting in a variety of greenish hues meant to camouflage stains. A lot of people had enjoyed a lot of cigarettes in there. I tossed my suitcase on the bed. Home sweet home.

I flipped open my cell phone and punched in Pete Strong's number before I realized there was no signal. I opened my suitcase and plugged in my netbook, but there wasn't any Wi-Fi, either. I used the room phone to call the front desk. Beulah answered on the second ring.

"May I help you?"

"This is Nicholas Colt in two oh eight. I can't find a jack in the wall for Internet access. Can I switch to another room? Nonsmoking, maybe?"

"I'm sorry, Mr. Colt, but none of our rooms have Internet access. We usually have a computer here at the lobby that is available to guests, but I'm afraid it's not working right now. Some kind of virus or something, the manager said. And we don't really have nonsmoking rooms. Sorry."

"I'm not getting any signal on my cell phone, either."

"Sorry, that's always a problem at this particular spot on the mountain. They're supposed to be putting up a new tower sometime soon. Least that's what I heard. I can give you a full refund now if you're not happy with the room."

"That's all right. Thank you."

I hung up. *Sorry* seemed to be the word of the day. But this was the only lodging anywhere near Black Creek, where Donna's brother had disappeared, so I was stuck with the primitive accommodations. I felt like Daniel Boone. I wondered if I would have to shoot a squirrel for dinner and rub two sticks together to get a fire going. I used my credit card to call Pete from the room phone.

"Strong Investigations."

"Pete, this is Nicholas Colt. Just got in."

"Hey, Nicholas. I'm on my way down there now. How was your trip?"

"Lots of trees and curvy roads."

"You should come up here in the fall sometime. It's quite spectacular."

"I can imagine. How far off are you?"

"Should be there in thirty minutes."

"Cool. I'm in room 208 at the motel."

"See you in a bit."

I stretched out on the bed and stared at the nicotine-stained ceiling.

CHAPTER FIVE

"Derek Wahl used to work in Nashville," Pete said.

We were sitting in a booth at Moe's Ribs. I'd told him about my history with the Harvest Angels three years ago.

A waitress named Millie kept giving Pete strange looks, as though serving coffee to an African-American man was a little bit more than she could take. Pete didn't show it, but I knew he must have been uncomfortable. The place was crawling with crew cuts, flannel shirts, and sour expressions.

"Derek was a cop in Nashville?" I said.

"Yeah, but he shot and killed a guy one night. Was never the same after that."

"You knew him?"

"I did a little research, talked to some guys he used to work with. It happened on the interstate one night. Guy named William Mullins in a Firebird doing eighty in a sixty-five. Derek paced him, then switched on the flashers. The Firebird sped up. Around the Kentucky border, it blew a tire and rolled and Mullins got out and hightailed it through a cornfield. When Derek caught up to him,

Mullins reached into his pocket and started to pull something out. Derek thought it was a gun. He fired one shot and killed the guy. The gun turned out to be a homemade crack pipe. Mullins was on probation, probably just wanted to ditch the pipe before Derek cuffed him."

"So Derek was terminated?"

"Resigned. The guys I talked to said he just couldn't take the stress of the city anymore. That's when he moved and took the job in Black Creek. But get this: Mullins was *from* Black Creek. Still had family there."

I motioned for Millie to bring us some more coffee. She came with a pot that looked like it might have been on the burner since breakfast. I stopped her before she filled our cups, and asked if she would mind bringing some that was freshly made. I asked politely.

"This is the freshest we got," she said.

"Then dump that forty-weight shit and make some more," I said.

She frowned. "It'll take about fifteen minutes."

"Great. Gives me something to look forward to."

I heard her say *some people* under her breath as she slogged back toward the kitchen.

Pete laughed. "The coffee really wasn't that bad."

"But fresh is better. For two bucks a cup, I don't think it's too much to ask."

"Mullins had a brother who didn't live far from the Lambs, where the double homicide took place," Pete said.

"What's the brother's name?"

"Harvey. Harvey Mullins. I even have an address for you."

"I'll check it out."

Pete lifted his briefcase, set it on the table, and opened it. "Here's the paperwork you'll need to work under my license while you're in Tennessee. I wish I could run the case with you, but I'm just too busy at the moment."

He handed me an envelope and a laminated ID card.

"Appreciate it. You ready to order some dinner?"

"I think I'll pass. I'm not feeling exactly welcome here, if you know what I mean."

"Fuck it, man. Let's eat."

"Next time you're in Nashville, give me a holler. I'll take you to a rib joint that makes this place look like a livestock trough."

"You're on, my friend."

We stood and shook hands. A few minutes after Pete left, Millie showed up with the fresh pot of coffee. She smiled. "Will it be just you for dinner tonight?"

I was starving. I hadn't eaten anything since I left Florida. I ordered a full rack of ribs and a baked potato and salad. There were some pies on display in a glass case on the counter, and I was already thinking about a slice of apple with a scoop of vanilla ice cream on top for dessert.

Millie took the menus from the table and Pete's empty coffee cup. When she walked past the counter, I heard one of the men sitting on a stool there say, "Better wash that one extra good, Millie."

"Wash it, hell," she said. "I'm going to throw it away."

Everyone got a good laugh. I cancelled my order and walked out.

CHAPTER SIX

I drove over to Piggly Wiggly and bought some things to keep in the room. Along with some groceries, I bought a Styrofoam cooler, a two-burner hotplate, a cheap saucepan, and a Teflon skillet. They had some steel coffee pots that looked like they came from the set of a cowboy movie, so I bought one of those and a big can of Folgers. I had decided to boycott Moe's, and I didn't feel like driving thirty miles every time I wanted something to eat. On the menu for tonight were pork and beans, olive loaf sandwiches, and a fried pie sealed in wax paper. I asked the stock boy where I could find some beer. He laughed and told me this was a dry county. I didn't think it was all that funny.

The sun had been gone for over an hour, and the yellow porch lights outside the motel rooms only added to the gloom. The mountain seemed darker than dark, an engulfing black hole that could suck you in and reduce you to molecules. I figured people who went missing around here probably stayed missing.

I carried my new things into the room, washed the saucepan and skillet, and set the hotplate on the long and narrow oak dresser.

I got some ice for the cooler and stowed my perishables. I opened a can of beans, dumped them into the saucepan, and dialed the heat to medium. I'd started putting a sandwich together when someone knocked on the door.

I looked through the peephole. A couple of guys stood there smoking cigarettes, trying their best to look tough. One fat, one skinny. The fat one wore a corduroy coat lined with sheepskin, and a Tennessee Titans skullcap. Late teens or early twenties. Chubby cheeks blistered red from the cold. The skinny guy was older, maybe in his midthirties. He wore a faded Levi's jacket over a hooded sweatshirt. A shiny silver hoop had been driven into the middle of his bottom lip.

My shirttails hid the little .38 strapped to my waist. I unlatched the deadbolt and opened the door. "Can I help you?"

"Mind if we come in for a minute?" the skinny one said.

"Who are you?"

"We work at Moe's. In the kitchen. I'm Lester, and this here's Earl."

"What do you want?"

"We just want to talk. We have some information you might be interested in. About the Harvest Angels."

They must have overhead me talking to Pete.

"The room's a mess," I said. "Hang on. Let me get my jacket and I'll step out there."

"Come on, mister. It's cold. And what we have to say needs to be said in private."

"Like I said, let me grab my coat and I'll—"

The fat one named Earl bulldozed into me, driving me backward into the room. I landed on my ass. He straddled me and pinned my wrists to the floor. He was enormous. I couldn't move.

"What the fuck you want?" I said.

"You talked mean to Millie," Earl said.

Lester lifted my beans from the hotplate, started eating directly from the pan with a spoon. He talked with his mouth full. "Who the hell you think you are, mister? You think you can come to our town and talk to us like dogs?"

"We were the ones being treated like dogs," I said.

The dump truck parked on my stomach made it difficult to breathe. Every time Earl shifted his fat ass, I almost blacked out.

Lester picked up my new ID from the bedside table. "Nicholas Colt. Special Investigator. Strong Investigations. You some kind of private eye, boy?"

I didn't say anything.

"My arms are getting tired," Earl said. "Can we go now?"

"We need to teach Mr. Colt here a lesson first."

"You said we was just going to scare him. I think we done did that."

Lester set my ID card back between the phone and the digital alarm clock. He carried the beans back to the hotplate, took one more bite before abandoning them. He reached into his pocket and pulled out a knife. He opened it, the blade locking into place with a click. He picked up the black leather jacket Juliet had bought me for Christmas the year before last, stabbed it violently in the back, and cut a slit all the way to the bottom seam.

"Next time, it ain't going to be your jacket." He put the knife away, walked over to where I lay helpless, and kicked me in the balls. "Let's go, Earl."

Earl got up and they walked out of the room and left me writhing on the floor.

CHAPTER SEVEN

The next morning I drove to Nashville and bought a new coat and a case of beer and another cooler. I took the beer to the motel room and dumped some ice on it from the ice machine. I ate four fried eggs and some bread and then headed to Black Creek.

I drove by two-story brick homes with columns in front and sprawling lawns and single-wide trailers with rusted skirting and makeshift porches and satellite dishes the size of spaceships. There were farms and abandoned filling stations and heavily treed gravel roads guarded by steel gates. On the radio, Billy Ray Cyrus sang about his achy breaky heart, but all I could think about were my achy breaky testicles. I was still sore from last night's trauma.

I planned to stop and have a talk with Harvey Mullins, but first I wanted to check out the Lambs' residence, where the murders had taken place. From the curb I saw a metal real estate sign in the front yard and a woman in her forties with bushy salt-and-pepper hair securing a lockbox to the cast-iron porch railing. When I got out and shut the door, she squinted my way and said, "Mr. Swanson? I was just about to give up on you."

"Sorry I'm late," I said, happy to be Mr. Swanson for a while if it granted me access to the home's interior.

"Hi, I'm Betty Johnson. I think you talked to Reba on the phone, but she had another place to show this morning."

"Pleased to meet you," I said.

She took the key back out of the lockbox and opened the front door. "Come on in. I think you're going to love this place."

We walked inside. Everything looked and smelled new. The walls and ceilings had been freshly painted, the oak floors sanded and refinished to a high gloss. Our voices and footsteps echoed as we made our way through the barren living room and into the kitchen.

"How many square feet?" I said.

"It's twelve hundred, but it feels bigger. Don't you think?"

"It does. What about the appliances?" The refrigerator, stove, and dishwasher were all brand new, all stainless steel, the manufacturer's stickers still on the handles.

"Everything stays. There's even a new washer and dryer." She opened a door and showed me the utility room.

"Nice," I said. "Is there a formal dining area?"

"In here."

We turned a corner to a short hallway and entered the room where Mrs. Lamb and her daughter-in-law had been butchered. All the evidence, of course, was long gone. The whole place looked as though it had been built yesterday.

"What happened to the previous owners?" I said.

"It was an elderly couple. They passed away."

"So who's selling the house?"

"Some great-niece or something. Their only heir. Reba could tell you more. Her name's Allison Parker. If you decide to buy the house, she's the one you'll be dealing with at closing."

I pulled a little spiral notepad out of my pocket. "Do you have Allison Parker's phone number?"

"I can't really give you her phone number. If you'd like to make an offer—"

"I'd just like to ask her a few questions."

"Well, if you give me *your* number, I can have her call you. How about that?"

"That's fine. I'm staying at the motel in Mont Falcon. Room two oh eight." Since cellular service in the area was so spotty, I wrote the motel's phone number down and tore the sheet from my notebook. I handed it to her.

"This says Nicholas Colt. I thought your name was—"

Someone pounded on the front door. Undoubtedly, the real Mr. Swanson.

—∽—

Harvey Mullins lived in a shotgun house near a set of railroad tracks. I doubted his place came with granite countertops and a Wolf gas range. Just a guess.

I walked to the door and rang the bell. The guy who answered held a can of Miller Lite in one hand and a cigarette in the other. He wore a wife-beater T and little or no deodorant.

"Are you Harvey Mullins?"

"Yeah. Who are you?"

I showed him my ID. "Nicholas Colt. I'm a private investigator."

"What do you want?"

I pulled an eight-by-ten photograph of Derek from an envelope. "You know who this is?"

"Yeah. It's the cop that killed my brother."

"He's missing. I was hired to find him."

"Yeah, yeah, the cops already talked to me. Long time ago. I don't know nothing about that. What, you think I killed those two women just to lure him into that house?"

"Stranger things have happened."

"Get the fuck off my porch."

"Look, I know you didn't have anything to do with those murders. You think I would come casually knocking on your door if I thought you were a suspect?"

"Then what do you want with me?"

"I wanted to ask if you'd ever had any contact with Derek. Seems strange he took a job in Black Creek, of all places, knowing the guy he shot had kin here."

His expression softened. "Come on in."

Fleece throw blankets covered the windows in Harvey's living room, effectively blocking any hint of sunlight. There was a tweed sofa, and a laptop computer surrounded by empty beer cans on a wooden coffee table. An infomercial about an exercise regimen blared from a plasma TV hugging the opposite wall. The furnace must have been cranked to eighty. Harvey motioned for me to have a seat, so I shrugged out of my new ski jacket and sat in the faux leather wingback chair next to the couch. A cloud of cigarette smoke hovered over a floor lamp with pictures of eagles on its shade.

Harvey switched off the television. "Can I get you a beer?"

"I'm good. Thanks."

"Let me just grab one real quick." He disappeared around the corner. I heard some bottles rattle when he opened the refrigerator. "Hey, you want some juice? I could make you a screwdriver."

"Maybe I'll take a beer after all." Rule #16 in Nicholas Colt's *Philosophy of Life*: Dedicated drinkers are always happier talking to their own kind.

Harvey brought the beers, sat on the sofa, and lit a Doral. "Yeah, so that cop Derek came over here one day with a Bible and some pamphlets about giving your heart to Jesus. He wanted me to pray with him."

"Did you?"

"Naw, you know, I'm not into it. I believe in God and everything, but I got no use for organized religion. You got your Catholics, your Jews, your Mormons, your Jehovah's Witnesses, Baptists, whatever. They all think their way is the right way. But they can't all be right, you know?"

"I know. So what kind of church did Derek go to?"

"Something weird. I can't remember the name."

"Do you still have the pamphlets?"

"Naw. I really didn't even like him coming into my house. He killed Billy, you know? I guess he thought he was going to make up for it by saving my soul. I wrote him a check for ten bucks just to get rid of him."

"Who did you make the check out to?"

Harvey snapped his fingers. He got up and walked through the archway to the kitchen, came back wearing a pair of reading glasses and flipping through the pages of a checkbook ledger.

"Here it is," he said. "New Love Ministries."

"Mind if I use your computer?"

"Go ahead."

I moved to the sofa, used Google to find the church's website. I wrote the address and phone number in my notebook.

"Want to go to church with me on Sunday?" I said.

"Naw. But you have fun, Mr. Colt."

"I'll try."

I sucked the beer can dry and set it on the coffee table with the other dead soldiers on my way out.

CHAPTER EIGHT

It was a clear and sunny Friday afternoon, twenty degrees and windless. The crisp February air felt good after the smothering heat and stench of Harvey's house. The radio weatherman said to expect warmer temperatures on Saturday with the possibility of snow.

When I got back to the motel, the light on my room phone was blinking. I called the front desk, and Beulah said a woman named Allison Parker had called. She gave me the number. I punched it in and got an answer on the fourth ring.

"This is Allison."

"Hi, this is Nicholas Colt. I looked at the house you have for sale earlier."

"Yes, the agent said you had some questions for me."

"Actually, it's not the house I'm interested in. I'm investigating the disappearance of Derek Wahl, the police officer who discovered the murders there."

"Oh, so you know about that."

"Yeah, I noticed Betty Johnson failed to mention it."

"It's not something we advertise. Hard enough to sell a house these days. Anyway, Derek Wahl is presumed dead, as are my uncle Virgil and cousin Joe. Normally it can take up to seven years to have a missing person legally declared dead, but the court accepted our petition to expedite because of the imminent peril—or something like that—of the situation. Bunch of legal mumbo jumbo. Anyway, it's the only reason I'm able to put the house up for sale. May I ask who you're working for, Mr. Colt?"

"My client wishes to remain anonymous."

"Of course. Well then, what can I help you with today?"

"Do you know who made the original nine-one-one call that Derek responded to?"

"It was from a prepaid cell phone. Untraceable. The police assumed it was one of the neighbors, although none of them would admit to it."

"My client said there was some DNA found at the scene that didn't belong to Derek or any of the Lambs. Do you know if the police ever got anywhere with that?"

"They found a little piece of rubber with a bloody fingerprint on it. They think it was from a mask the killer was wearing, but the print didn't match up with any of their databases and neither did the DNA from the blood. That's what they told me, anyway."

"Were you close to your aunt and uncle?"

"Not at all. I only knew them from family reunions when I was a kid. But if you think I might have had something to do with killing them, you're barking up the wrong tree. I don't stand to gain anything from the sale of that house. I'm just trying to cover some of their debts."

"What kind of debts?"

"Uncle Virgil was a gambler. Always had been. He and Aunt Martha should have owned that place free and clear a long time ago, but he kept getting equity loans to feed his habit. It's a wonder they didn't end up on the street."

"What was his game?"

"Pardon me?"

"Most hardcore gamblers have a favorite thing they like to bet on. I'm guessing there aren't any casinos around here, so I was just wondering—"

"He did it all. His idea of a big vacation was driving up to Louisville and hanging around the track for a couple of weeks. He bet on sports events, played the lotto, whatever. Some of the people I talked to when I was getting the house ready to sell said he'd been into poker lately. There was a game he went to every Friday night."

"Big stakes?"

"I don't know. Couldn't have been too big, I guess. Uncle Virgil was on a fixed income, and the house was mortgaged to the hilt. I just don't see how he could have had much money to play with at this point."

"Banks aren't the only way to borrow money. Any idea where the poker game was?"

"No, but I know where you can probably find out. Uncle Virgil had a friend there in Black Creek named Mike Musselman. Been friends since they were kids. I'm sure they knew each other's secrets. I'm also sure the police have already worked that angle."

"Probably, but I'll check into it. You've been very helpful, Ms. Parker. I appreciate your time."

"No problem. Good luck with your investigation."

After we said good-bye, I called information and asked for Mike Musselman's number, which turned out to be unlisted. I ate a sandwich and drank a beer and wondered how anyone ever got anything done before the Internet was invented. I put my jacket on, went outside, and walked around to the office. Beulah was asleep in a chair, a thread of drool dangling from her bottom lip. I fed some coins into the vending machine and pushed button number twelve and a deck of playing cards clanked into the steel receiving tray below. I broke the seal, pulled out the jokers, started shuffling the remaining fifty-two, hoping the noise would wake Beulah. It did not. I found the countertop service bell behind a bowl of candy canes left over from Christmas. I dinged it with my palm. Beulah's eyes fluttered open and she wiped her mouth on her shirtsleeve.

"Can I help you?"

"Sorry to bother you. I was just wondering if there was anything to do around here on a Friday night."

"What did you have in mind?"

"Is there a movie theater nearby?"

"Nashville. You like basketball?"

I shrugged. "Sure."

"There's a game over at the high school tonight. It's only three bucks to get in, and those boys can really play. State champs last year."

"Sounds great. Or maybe I'll just hang around the room and play some solitaire. Hey, you know anyone who might like to get up a card game?"

"Well, I ain't too busy right now. I could play you a game of rummy." Her smile showed some teeth missing.

"I was thinking more along the lines of some seven card stud. You know, for money. But thanks anyway."

I started to walk out.

"Poker?" she said. "I might be able to set you up with something."

That's what I wanted to hear.

CHAPTER NINE

I filled up at Sunoco and got four hundred dollars from the ATM. I'd spoken on the phone to a man named Ted Grayson, who said they just happened to have a seat open for the game tonight. Dollar ante, five-card draw with jacks or better and a ten-dollar limit on raises. I figured four hundred would last me at least a few hours.

Slick patches of ice pocked the narrow gravel incline leading to Ted's house, and I almost got stuck a couple of times. I finally made it up the hill and pulled into a slot next to the four-car garage. Everyone else parked there had pickup trucks with big tires. There was a wooden staircase mounted to the side of the building. I climbed it and knocked. A man with slicked-back silver hair and a goatee answered.

"You Nicholas?"

"That's me."

"Ted Grayson. Come on in."

The upstairs had been converted into an efficiency apartment. Galley kitchen, sofa and love seat, big-screen TV. There was a large round table in the middle of the room and five whiskey barrels that had died and come back as chairs. Ted introduced me to the men occupying three of them. "This here's Chris Waite, Garland Yokum, and Bobby Greer."

I nodded. "Gentlemen."

"Take your coat off, fix yourself a drink. We'll be done with this hand in a minute and then we'll deal you in."

"Thanks."

I hung my coat on a rack in the corner, walked to the kitchen, and poured two fingers of Maker's Mark bourbon over some ice cubes. I sat on a stool and watched the game. Nobody was smoking, and there were no drinks on the table. The room was quiet except for the occasional *kick you five* and the clattering of chips added to the pile. No laughing and joking, no side conversations about football or race cars or women. I got the feeling I wasn't going to get any information from these guys. They had come for a serious game of poker, and nothing else. I decided to relax and enjoy myself and try to win some money.

Chris folded first, and then Bobby. After the three-raise maximum, Ted and Garland showed their hands and Garland took the pot with queens over deuces.

"You get more boats than the goddamn Navy," Ted said. "Come on, Nicholas."

I set my whiskey glass on the counter and slid into the vacant chair at the table. I bought two hundred dollars' worth of chips. We all anted, and Ted dealt the hand.

I got a pair of aces and opened with five dollars, which Garland immediately bumped to ten. He had a lot of chips and was playing aggressively. Everyone discarded, and Ted passed the new cards around. I got a third ace and a seven and a king. It was Garland's bet. He bet ten and I raised him ten and Chris raised another ten after that. Nobody folded. There was over two hundred dollars in the pot.

"Call," I said, tossing another blue chip onto the pile.

"Two pair," Chris said. "Pair of fives and another pair of fives."

He fanned the cards on the table for everyone to see. He had four of a kind, which beats everything but a straight flush. He hooked his arm around the pot and started to rake the sizeable mound his way.

"Hold on," Garland said. "You called two pair."

"It was a joke," Chris said. "You seen my hand."

"Nobody's laughing. You called two pair, so that's what you have."

"Come on, Garland," Ted said. "Give the guy his pot. He won it fair and square."

"Bullshit, man." Garland spread his cards out. "I got a ten-high straight. I believe that beats two pair."

"Dude, be reasonable," Chris said.

"Face it, man. You fucked up."

"OK, I fucked up. But it's still my pot. Give me a break. This is the first time in my life I ever got—"

Someone banged on the door.

From Garland's direction came a click that could only have been the hammer of a handgun being pulled back. "You expecting someone, Ted?"

Ted went to the door and looked through the peephole. "It's just Mike."

He opened the door and a tall elderly man stepped in wearing a long wool coat and a hat made from black fur. He looked like he had gotten off a plane from Moscow in 1959. "Damn, it's cold out there," he said, his accent anything but Russian.

"Thought you couldn't make it tonight," Ted said. "We already got a fifth player."

Mike squinted toward the table, his eyes still adjusting to the brightness of the room. He pulled off his gloves, which appeared to be lined with the same fur that adorned his headgear. "Who's that?"

"Nicholas Colt. Out-of-towner. He's all right. Beulah over at the motel vouched for him. Nicholas, this here's Mike Musselman."

"Pleased to meet you," I said. I kept Garland in my peripheral vision. His hands were still under the table.

"Maybe you can settle a little dispute we have going here," Ted said. He explained the situation to Mike.

"Technically, Garland is correct," Mike said. "If you call two pair, then that's what you have. But we're all friends here, right fellas?"

"I reckon," Garland said. He reached down and slid his gun back into his boot. It made me nervous that nobody seemed to find this unusual. Chris raked the chips to his side of the table and started organizing them into stacks.

"I can sit out if you want to play a hand," I said to Mike. I wanted to talk to him about Virgil Lamb, but this was neither the time nor the place.

"Well, if you're sure," Mike said.

"I'm sure."

I went to the kitchen, took a sip of my drink. Ted shuffled the cards while Mike took off his KGB costume. He was totally bald on top, with just a fringe of closely cropped gray hair on the sides.

"Anybody got a cigarette?" I asked.

Bobby reached into his pocket and pulled out a pack of Winstons. "You'll have to go outside," he said. "Ted don't allow no smoking up here."

"Appreciate it." I walked over and pulled a cigarette from the pack.

"Need a light?" Chris handed me a green disposable lighter.

"Thanks. Be right back."

I grabbed my jacket from the brass coatrack and walked outside and down the stairs. I scanned the cigarette across my nostrils, absorbing its bouquet. I put it in my mouth and drew a lungful of frigid air through it. It tasted heavenly. I was tempted to light it. I wanted to. I broke it and threw it on the ground.

There was an older model Chevy Silverado parked behind one of the other trucks. It hadn't been there earlier, so I knew it belonged to Mike Musselman. I reached into my pocket and pulled out the Mini Maglite I keep on my keychain. I switched it on and shined the light into Mike's interior, careful to avoid touching the truck and possibly tripping an alarm. There were some Styrofoam cups on the passenger's side floorboard from places like McDonald's and Hardee's and Dunkin' Donuts. There was a cell phone on the console and a pair of sunglasses. The seat had a small rip on the driver's side with some stuffing poking out.

I walked around to the rear of the truck and memorized the license plate. If I could talk Beulah into letting me use the motel's computer for a few minutes, it wouldn't be hard to find Mike's address by cross-referencing the tag number. I wanted to watch his house for a couple of days. Maybe he and his buddy Virgil used the same loan shark. I still needed to check out New Love Ministries, but I had a hunch Derek Wahl had walked into a situation that had nothing to do with him personally. Wrong place, wrong time.

I figured Virgil Lamb and Derek Wahl and Virgil's grandson Joe Lamb were all dead, but I wanted to find out whatever I could to give Donna some closure. I was having serious doubts that the Harvest Angels had had anything to do with anything. Juliet was probably right. The killings were probably done by a copycat, a loan shark's hired muscle trying to throw suspicion elsewhere.

Thinking about Juliet reminded me I needed to call home. I checked my cell phone for a signal, saw that I had two bars, started to punch the speed dial for Juliet's number when a voice behind me said, "Looking for something?"

It was Chris. He had somehow made it down the stairs without me hearing him. He had an unlit cigarette stuck in his mouth.

"I used to own a truck like this," I said. "I was just checking it out."

"Can I have my lighter?"

I handed it to him. "I'm going to head back up."

"Who were you calling?"

"My wife. I can't get a signal over at the motel."

"Oh."

"She didn't answer. I'll try again later."

I walked around to the staircase and climbed back up to the apartment. Ted and Bobby and Garland and Mike were taking a break in the kitchen.

"What you drinking?" Ted asked.

"Maker's," I said. "On the rocks."

He took a fresh glass from the cupboard, plunked a couple of ice cubes in it, filled it halfway with whiskey, and handed it to me.

"I make my ice cubes with Evian," he said. "From the French Alps. Best water in the world. I can't stand chlorine. Ruins the taste of good liquor."

"Damn good ice," I said.

"And that glass you're drinking from is Waterford crystal. Seventy-five dollars apiece. I like having nice things. I like having the best."

I swirled the bourbon, causing the ice to make elegant little tinkling sounds. "You certainly have exquisite taste. What kind of business are you in?"

They all laughed.

"You're joking, right?" Ted said.

"No, really. I've been wondering what people around here do for a living."

"A lot of them work for me. I own a meat-processing plant. Grayson's Meats. Maybe you've heard of it."

"Yeah, I have some of your bologna and olive loaf back at the motel. I just didn't make the connection. I don't think we have that brand in Florida."

"We distribute in Tennessee, Kentucky, and Ohio. For now. But we're planning to expand. How about you, Nicholas? What kind of work do you do?"

"I'm a musician. I had a band in the eighties called Colt Forty-Five. Southern rock and blues."

Ted snapped his fingers. "Nicholas Colt. Hot damn, I thought the name sounded familiar. I have some of your records, man."

"You still playing?" Bobby asked.

"I have a little blues band. We play at a club in Jacksonville."

"I remember when the airplane went down," Ted said. "Terrible. Just terrible. So what brings you to Tennessee?"

The possibility that another Harvest Angels cell existed had brought me to Tennessee, but I didn't tell Ted that.

"I'm scouting fishing locations for spring," I said. "If it ever gets here."

"You must be some kind of serious fisherman."

My stepfather had taught me how to shoot a gun, and he taught me how to fish. Those were the things we did on the rare occasions he wasn't too drunk to stand up. We never went to the movies and we never played catch and we never stepped foot inside a church. We fished and we shot guns. So I guess Ted was right. I guess I was some kind of serious fisherman. I guess I'd been one most of my life.

I thought about the pamphlet I'd looked at when I first got to the Mont Falcon motel and said, "I'm planning on taking home the twenty-five-thousand-dollar first prize at the Lake Timberland bass rodeo. You can't just show up and expect to do well. You need a plan, plenty of prep time. Plus, it's an excuse to get away from the old lady for a few days. If you know what I mean."

Ted chuckled. "Sure do. What kind of boat do you have?"

"Ranger Z Intracoastal," I lied. "With a two-fifty Yamaha."

"Damn. That's a serious boat, all right. Well, good luck with the tournament."

"Thanks." I looked at my watch. "Listen, guys, I hate to be a party pooper—"

Chris opened the door. A blast of cold air whooshed in behind him. "What the fuck?" he said. He was holding the broken cigarette I'd left on the ground. He came in and tossed it on the counter.

"I can explain that," I said, trying my best to remain calm.

"He was out there nosing around Mike's truck," Chris said. "I saw him shine a flashlight through the window, and then he walked around to the tailgate and checked the license number. He just used the cigarette as an excuse to go outside."

"Like I told you, I used to own a truck like that. I was just looking it over. I walked to the rear to see what kind of tow package it had. As for the cigarette, I quit a couple of years ago, but I still have major cravings sometimes. I broke it and threw it away so I wouldn't be tempted to light it."

"Chris, this here's Nicholas Colt from the band Colt Forty-Five," Ted said. "You're probably too young to remember them, but they were big back in the day. Real big. Quit being so goddamn paranoid, boy. Every time a stranger comes to town—"

"I'm telling you, he's up to something," Chris said. "I don't trust him, not one bit."

"I'll be leaving now, gentlemen," I said. "Cash me in, Ted."

"It's early. Come on, let's play."

"Really. Cash me in."

"If you insist. Hey, if I walk over to the house and get one of your albums, would you mind signing it for me?"

—⁓—

Before I started the Camry and left Ted's driveway, I called Juliet from my cell phone. From the sound of her voice, I could tell she had been crying.

"What's wrong?" I said.

"What's *not* wrong is more like it. The washing machine quit working. It won't even come on, so I have a pile of laundry a mile high. No clean uniforms for work tomorrow night. I drove all the way over to Green Cove and waited in line for an hour to get my driver's license renewed, only to find out you have to have a ton of documents proving your identity now. So I have to get all that together and go back and spend another day dealing with *that* crap."

"Did you call someone about the washing machine?"

"Yeah, it's still under warranty, but they're not going to come and look at it til Monday. I guess I'll have to go to the Laundromat tomorrow, like I really have time. And Brittney is driving me nuts. Can I just go ahead and let her drive? I don't think I can handle this for one more day, much less two weeks."

"I don't think it would set a very good precedent to let her go ahead and drive," I said. "She needs to finish out her two weeks."

"Then you need to come home and deal with her. You need to throw your shit in the car and come home *now*, before I totally lose my mind."

"I can't come home right now. I have a couple more leads I need to follow up on."

"There's absolutely no reason for you to be up there, Nicholas. Why are you? Because you're obsessed with that Christian militia group?"

"I'm not obsessed with anything," I said.

But I was. The Harvest Angels were responsible for the plane crash that killed my wife, Susan, and daughter, Harmony. Susan was from Jamaica. We were an interracial couple, and I was famous. We were on the cover of *Rolling Stone* magazine as bride and groom. Susan and Harmony died because of their skin color. I was the sole survivor. Twenty years after the crash, I found out it wasn't an accident. I found out while tracking a fifteen-year-old runaway who ended up becoming my adopted daughter. To say I was obsessed was an understatement.

"You don't even know it was them," Juliet said.

"But I'm here, and I'm going to find out."

She hung up. I tried to call her back, got voice mail. I left a message telling her to check the circuit breaker for the washing machine. I had a hunch that was the problem. Washing machines don't usually die completely without warning like that.

I started the car and drove back to the motel.

CHAPTER TEN

I got up Saturday morning and started a pot of coffee and tried to call Juliet from the room phone. She still wasn't answering. I tried Brittney's number, got voice mail the first two times. I tried again and she finally picked up.

"Daddy?"

"Hi, sweetheart."

"What time is it?"

"A little after ten," I said. "You still asleep?"

"Yeah."

"Sorry. Just wanted to check on you guys."

She yawned. "We're fine, I guess. When are you coming home?"

"Soon. Is your mom around?"

"She goes to the gym on Saturdays."

"That's right. I forgot. I'll try to call her later."

"Are you having fun up there?"

"A blast. I think it's about eighteen degrees outside this morning."

"That sucks," she said.

"Yeah."

"It's warmed up some down here. Supposed to be in the sixties today."

"I'll be glad to get home. All right, you go on back to sleep if you want. Love you."

"Love you too. I'd love you even more if you'd let me drive."

"Bye," I said.

"Bye."

I ate some breakfast and then walked to the lobby. The sky was heavy with swollen clouds the color of molten lead. The ski jacket I'd bought kept my upper body warm enough, but my legs were cold and stiff and my knees ached. I could have used some long underwear. I made a mental note to stop somewhere and buy some.

Beulah was at the desk.

"Finding some good fishing spots?" she said.

She must have seen me looking at the pamphlet, or maybe she'd talked to Ted Grayson.

"A couple," I said.

"Spring is just around the corner. Hope you'll come back and stay with us."

"Only if you're still here."

She blushed. "Why, Mr. Colt. You make an old woman's heart flutter."

"We'll have to play that game of rummy sometime," I said.

"Promise?"

"Promise. Hey, would you mind if I got on your computer for just a minute?"

"Oh, we're not allowed to let guests—"

"Just for a minute. Less than a minute."

"Well…"

I walked around the counter. Beulah stepped aside and gave me access to her keyboard and monitor. Thirty seconds later, I had a printout with information on Virgil Lamb's friend Mike Musselman.

"Thanks," I said. "You have a great morning, Beulah."

"You too, Mr. Colt."

"You can call me Nicholas."

She blushed again.

—m—

The fact sheet I had on Mike Musselman said he was eighty-three years old, but he looked a couple of decades younger than that. He answered the door holding a glass of something orange.

"Can I help you?" he said.

"It's Nicholas Colt," I said. "From the card game."

"Oh. Can I help you?" He was trying to be polite, but he had a *what-the-hell-do-you-want* expression on his face. I held my ground.

"I just wanted to talk to you for a few minutes," I said.

"About?"

I showed him my PI license, looked him directly in the eyes. "About Virgil Lamb," I said.

He hesitated, examined his New Balance sneakers for a second, shrugged, and said, "All right. Come on in."

There was a stationary bicycle and a set of dumbbells situated in one corner of his living room. I sat on one end of a denim sofa, and Mike sat in a gray and black swivel chair by his computer desk. There was a large cage beside the desk with a bird in it. The bird was white with a yellow head and bright orange circles under its eyes

"Get you something to drink?" Mike said.

"What's that in your glass?"

"Carrot juice. Want some?"

"No thanks," I said. "I wanted to talk to you about your friend. It won't take long."

"Virgil Lamb was the best friend I ever had. I was pretty devastated when he went missing last year. It was like losing an arm or something, you know? Part of me was just suddenly gone."

"I'm sure he is missed by many," I said.

"So why are you investigating Virgil?"

The bird squawked.

"I was hired by Derek Wahl's sister to investigate the crimes at the Lambs' residence a year ago Thanksgiving," I said. "There were crosses carved into the victims' foreheads, same as the one on my adopted daughter's sister three years ago. I know who killed Leitha. He's dead now. He was involved in a Christian militia group called the Harvest Angels."

"So you've connected some dots, and you're assuming whoever was responsible for the Lamb murders was also involved in this Christian militia group. What was it called?"

"Harvest Angels. It was the militant branch of a cult called Chain of Light. I'm not assuming anything, just trying to rule it out at this point. Ever heard of New Love Ministries? Supposedly that's where Derek went to church."

"They have a billboard out on the highway. They run ads in the local paper sometimes. I don't know anything about them."

"Do you know if Virgil might have gotten involved with them?"

"Never in a million years. He hated religion."

"What did Virgil do for a living?" I said. "You know, before he retired."

"You don't know?"

"No."

"He was The Great Masserto," Mike said. "I was Miguel the Magician, and Virgil was The Great Masserto. We were in a traveling show called Captain Lucky's Entertainment Extravaganza and Thrill Theatre."

"You were magicians?"

"*I* was a magician. Virgil was a psychic and a hypnotist, the best there ever was. He had an offer for a television show one time, but the deal fell through. They ended up giving the show to a guy named Kreskin."

"*The Amazing World of Kreskin*," I said. "I remember that show. Sometime in the seventies."

"Yeah. Kreskin was a few years younger than us, but Virgil was ten times more talented."

"How did you guys end up in that line of work?"

"You really want to know?"

"Sure."

"A guy from *Life* magazine wrote an article about it one time. I can print you a copy."

"That would be great," I said. "What kind of bird is that?"

"Cockatiel. His name is Waldo."

"Can he talk?"

"When he wants to."

I got up and walked to the cage. Waldo cocked his head and eyeballed me. He didn't say anything.

"I understand Virgil was quite the gambler," I said.

"It was his only vice. He didn't drink or smoke or take drugs, but he sure liked to bet money."

"How did he do with it?" I said.

"What are you getting at, Mr. Colt?"

"I think you know what I'm getting at. Did he owe someone a large sum of money? Did he get himself and everyone in that house killed because of it?"

"The police asked me the same thing," Mike said.

"And what did you tell them?"

"I told them I didn't pry into Virgil Lamb's financial affairs."

"Come on, Mike. Just tell me. Did he ever use a loan shark to raise money to gamble with?"

He looked up at me from his desk chair. His eyes were bloodshot. "Only once that I know of," he said. "And don't ask me for a name."

"Because you don't know? Or because you're not going to tell me?"

"I can't tell you. They'll kill me if I tell you."

I saw the fear in Mike Musselman's eyes, and that was good enough for me. Virgil Lamb had gotten in over his head with some very violent people. He and his family were murdered because of a gambling debt. Derek Wahl was dispatched to the residence based on an anonymous call to the police, and when he showed up the bad guys had to kill him as well. That was my guess. Other than the crosses carved on the victims' foreheads, there was no evidence that a Harvest Angels cell existed in this part of the country. And if the Harvest Angels weren't involved in the killings, then I was done in Tennessee.

"Thanks for your time," I said.

Mike got up and walked me to the door. He handed me the papers he had printed out from the *Life* magazine archives. The article was from August 11, 1961.

"I'm eighty-three," he said, "but I still like living. I'm still thankful for every day I have."

"Take care," I said.

I stepped out onto the stoop. Just before Mike closed the door, Waldo said, "Kiss my ass."

Stupid bird.

CHAPTER ELEVEN

I had one more box to check off before going home. I drove to the New Love Ministries church Sunday morning. I had planned to attend the service until I saw that many of the worshippers entering the building were black. New Love was obviously not affiliated with the Harvest Angels, so that was that.

I drove back to the motel, crammed all my things into the Camry, walked to the office and handed over my room key. I told the clerk on duty to tell Beulah I said good-bye.

The tilted crosses carved into the foreheads of the murder victims at the Lambs' residence were some sick bastard's idea of a joke, a bogus clue that would have homicide detectives chasing their tails and looking in all the wrong places. Virgil Lamb had gotten in over his head with gambling debt, and Derek had simply been collateral damage. He was probably wearing some very heavy shoes at the bottom of a very deep river now.

I made it home a little after six. I hadn't called ahead. I thought I would make it a surprise. My Jimmy was in the driveway, parked exactly where I'd left it. I opened the driver's side door and checked the odometer. It hadn't moved. The garage door was open. Juliet's car was parked in there. I walked through the garage, opened the entrance to the kitchen, stepped inside, and said, "Anybody home?"

For some reason, I'd pictured Juliet and Brittney sitting at the dinette looking fretful. In my fantasy they saw that I'd come home earlier than expected and relief flooded their faces and they jumped up and ran to me in slow motion. They embraced me and smothered me with kisses, and we all lived happily ever after. Like some kind of greeting-card commercial.

But that's not what happened.

There was a partially eaten bowl of chicken noodle soup on the table and a package of saltines. There was a book titled *212* by Alafair Burke next to the bowl of soup, opened to page 147. There was a smear of blood on the table next to the book, and drops of blood leading to the hallway.

Another one of Brittney's nosebleeds, I told myself.

I followed the trail to the master bedroom. I opened the door. Juliet and Brittney sat side by side on the bed, their backs cushioned by pillows against the headboard. They stared blankly at the television. Their faces were the color of raw biscuit dough. Their lips were blue. They had been gagged with pillowcases and bound with duct tape, and their hair in front was matted with coagulated blood

I couldn't breathe. High-pitched sobs emanated from the back of my throat, as though I were in a nightmare and couldn't wake up. My legs turned to putty. I leaned against the doorjamb to keep from falling. *This can't be happening. Not again. Please, dear God, not again.*

Brittney moaned, and a raspy breath escaped from Juliet's chest. They were in shock, still alive but in dire need of medical attention. I quickly helped them into lying positions and propped pillows under their legs. I untied the gags and pulled the comforter up to keep them warm. There was a telephone on the bedside table, and I had started toward it when I heard footsteps coming up the hallway.

Someone was still in the house.

I turned and saw him coming at me fast with a large knife from the kitchen. He was dressed in black. He had a ski mask pulled over his head, and all I could see were a pair of pale gray eyes focused on my throat.

A rush of adrenaline flooded through me, and I was able to dodge the first thrust. I reached for my .38. It wasn't there. I had taken it back to the Airstream on my way in. I stood face-to-face with the killer now as he continuously swiped at me with the razor-sharp blade.

He moved forward relentlessly, inch by inch, backing me toward the wall. I kept my eyes on the knife. I recognized it from our cutlery block. You could cut a slice of ham thin as paper with it. I knew, because I had put the edge on it myself with an oilstone. The stone had belonged to my stepfather. It was one of two things I inherited at fifteen when he committed suicide. The other thing was the .44 Magnum he had used to blow his own brains out. I'd had the gun melted down to a blob, and it rests in peace on my desk alongside my mother's ill-fated St. Christopher statue.

Thinking about it triggered another memory.

The killer lunged forward like a pirate in a swordfight. I spun right, and the knife went deep into the drywall. It took him a second to dislodge it, enough time for me to drop to the floor and roll toward the bed. I reached under the sham and quickly unsnapped the holster I'd strapped to the frame. As the man who had obviously intended to slaughter my family came at me overhand with the ten-inch blade, I pulled the .357 from its leather seat and blasted four enormous holes in his torso. The bullets exited through his back, leaving chunks of flesh and blood splatters on the wall behind him.

He dropped the knife and collapsed. He was done. I crawled to him and yanked off the ski mask.

At first, I couldn't quite process the image. When I finally did, my heart lurched and a black curtain closed on my peripheral vision. I almost passed out.

It was Derek Wahl.

I recognized him from the pictures Donna had given me.

I staggered to the phone and dialed 9-1-1.

CHAPTER TWELVE

Juliet and Brittney were transported to the hospital via helicopter. Their treatment in the emergency department included a consultation with a plastic surgeon to stitch the cuts on their foreheads.

The tilted crosses.

They were admitted to the trauma unit on the eighth floor, where they shared a semiprivate room. They had suffered some blunt trauma to their skulls along with the cuts, but they were stable. X-rays negative for any brain swelling, the doctor had said. I sat there and watched them sleep for a while. There was an armed guard posted outside their door.

I sat there until a deputy from the sheriff's department came and motioned me out to the hallway. At his request, I left the hospital and met Donna at the Clay County morgue where she positively identified Derek's body. Donna had asked for me. She wanted me there. She wanted me to get a good look at him lying on the slab with four black holes in his chest.

An autopsy had been scheduled, as a matter of protocol. Not that there was any doubt about the cause of death.

I was wiped out. Numb. I walked Donna to her car. She was crying.

"Why did you have to kill him?" she said. "Couldn't you have just shot him in the leg or something?"

"He was coming at me with a knife. I—"

"He obviously wasn't in his right mind. An eye for an eye, right? Is that what you were thinking when you shredded his body with that hand cannon?"

"I wasn't thinking anything. I was reacting to the situation. And I didn't know it was Derek, for that matter. He had a mask on."

"I'm going to see that you pay for this, Nicholas. One way or another, I'm going to see that you pay."

She climbed into her car, started the engine, and drove away.

—∞—

It was ten o'clock by the time I made it back up to the trauma unit. I got off the elevator and followed the signs. I hadn't learned the layout of the place yet. The hallway lights had been dimmed. Everything looked green and creepy, like the inside of an aquarium. There was a different armed guard posted outside room 834.

"Can I help you, sir?"

"I'm family," I said.

"What relation?"

"I'm the husband. And the father."

"Could I see some identification, please?"

I showed him my driver's license. He checked my name against a list on a clipboard and waved me in. Only a few minutes, he said. Visiting hours had ended at nine.

Brittney was still sleeping. She looked comfortable. Juliet's eyes opened when she heard me come in. I lifted a small padded chair and quietly placed it next to her bed.

"Hi, babe," I said.

"Hi."

"How are you?"

"Terrible. I look like the bride of Frankenstein."

"Believe me, you look great. The scar will fade. The surgeon said so."

"I guess I could always wear bangs," she said, her lips curling into the faintest hint of a smile.

"I'm so sorry this happened," I said.

"He came in through the garage. He hid by the washer and dryer and waited for me to come and tend to the laundry."

She told me as many details as she could remember. "If you hadn't come when you did, he would have killed us."

"I know."

"Why did he want to kill us?"

"I don't know."

I didn't know much of anything at that point, but I was determined to get to the bottom of it all. I was determined to find out why Derek Wahl had disappeared for over a year, and why he had shown up in Florida and tried to kill my wife and daughter. Was Derek connected to the Harvest Angels? Were the tilted crosses some sort of calling card, as I had surmised before? Was Derek responsible for the deaths at the Lambs' residence and the disappearance of Virgil Lamb and his grandson Joe? Those were the some of the questions stewing in the back of my mind, cooking on simmer while I sat there and talked to Juliet.

"Will there be others?" she said. "Will others come and try to kill us?"

"We're not going to take any chances. As soon as you and Brittney are discharged from the hospital, the two of you are flying to the Philippines to stay with your family for a while. I've already made the arrangements."

"But I have work. Brittney has school. We can't just—"

"None of that matters. You can take a leave of absence, and I'm sure the good folks at Brittney's school will be happy to let her do some work online once I explain the situation. I'm going to get to the bottom of this, Jules. Hopefully it won't take too long."

"I guess a trip home would be nice. Mom and Dad haven't even met Brittney yet."

"That's the spirit," I said, not bothering to correct her. Juliet's parents had flown in for our wedding, and had briefly met Brittney then. The ER doctor had told me there might be some amnesia from the injuries, from the beatings and the lacerations. He said it would be temporary.

"Can you stay here with us tonight?" Juliet said.

"They won't let me."

"But I'll be afraid."

"There's a guard outside your door. He has a gun."

"It's not the bad guys I'm afraid of. It's the nurses."

This time her smile was genuine.

"I love you," I said.

"I love you, too."

CHAPTER THIRTEEN

Four days later Juliet and Brittney were on the long flight to Manila, and I was back at my old room in Mont Falcon. I thought Beulah was going to try to hug me when I walked into the office. Long-lost pals, old Beul and me.

It was Wednesday, February 24. Derek Wahl's memorial service was scheduled for Friday. I wasn't going to make it. I didn't think I would be welcome anyway. I sent Donna a check, reimbursing her for the money she had given me to find him. I refunded every bit of it, even though I could account for at least half in expenses.

The sheriff's department had exonerated me from any wrong-doing, ruling the shooting self-defense, but I had a feeling Donna might try to file some sort of civil suit. Maybe refunding the retainer would cause her to reconsider. Maybe not. At any rate, I was operating on my own dime now, and there was something very liberating about that.

Moe's Ribs closed at 11:00 p.m. At 11:32, Lester and Earl came out the back door. Earl was the fat one. He lit a joint, took a long hit, and passed it to Lester. I was standing beside the Dumpster. They walked by without noticing me.

"Hey, fellas," I said. "Remember me?"

They turned. Lester cuffed the joint, a habit among potheads when they're startled. It's automatic, the way a dog's ears perk if you snap your fingers.

"Hold this," Lester said.

He handed the joint to Earl. He reached into his pocket and pulled out his knife. I reached under my shirttail and pulled out my .38.

"Take a walk, fat boy," I said.

I didn't have to say it twice. Earl abandoned his friend like a bad plate of fish. He sauntered away with the marijuana cigarette smoldering between his chubby fingers.

Lester was the one I wanted to talk to. He seemed to have a few more IQ points than Earl, and I didn't want to deal with them both again if things got physical.

"Throw the knife in there," I said, gesturing toward the Dumpster.

"This here knife cost a hundred bucks, mister."

"In that case, close it and set it on the ground."

He closed it and set it on the ground. I told him to lace his fingers behind his head and take four steps backward and get on his knees. He did. I walked to the knife and picked it up and put it in my pocket.

"Oh, I see how it is," he said. "You're a goddamn thief."

"This doesn't even come close to covering the cost of my jacket," I said. "The way I see it, you owe me about three hundred more dollars."

"You're quite the badass with that gun in your hand. What are you going to do now, execute me?"

I holstered the revolver. "Stand up."

There was a board from a broken pallet beside the Dumpster with some rusty nails sticking out of one end. Lester grabbed it on his way up and came at me with it raised over his head like a club. I blocked the blow with my left forearm and buried my right fist deep into his solar plexus. He doubled over and dropped the board and fell to the pavement, curling into a fetal position next to some stray rubbish.

"What do you know about the Harvest Angels?" I said.

He didn't say anything. He was having a little trouble breathing.

"I know you know something, because you mentioned them the night you came knocking on my door with your morbidly obese friend."

At first, I thought they had overheard Pete and me talking about the Harvest Angels at our table at Moe's ribs. At first I thought that was all there was to it. But dishwashers don't generally come to your room and assault you and vandalize your property just for having a few harsh words with a waitress. I had a hunch there was more to it than that, and my hunch turned out to be right.

"I've heard of them," Lester said.

"What have you heard?"

He grunted. "I think you busted something inside me, mister. I need a doctor."

"What have you heard?" I said, louder and more emphatic than the first time.

"I got drunk one night with a guy who said he was a member."

"What's his name?"

"Bear. Everybody calls him Bear. He's a big guy."

"What's his last name?"

"I don't know."

"Where can I find him?"

"Ain't seen him around in a while."

"Where was he when you did see him?"

"There's a little shack over off Carp Lane where guys hang out and drink and watch football and stuff. Everyone just calls it The Bar."

"I thought this was a dry county," I said.

"I didn't say it was legal."

"What else have you heard?"

"Nothing."

"You sure?"

"I swear, man."

I leaned over and grabbed his lip ring between my thumb and forefinger, and gave it a quick jerk. He screamed. Blood gushed from his chunk of mouth that wasn't there anymore.

"That's for kicking me in the balls," I said.

He was punching some numbers into his cell phone as I walked away.

CHAPTER FOURTEEN

Thursday morning I drove up to Nashville and got lost looking for Pete Strong's office. I finally found it. It was a little gray box of a house on Forty-Seventh Avenue North with a strip of gravel in front for parking. Not quite what I had expected.

There was an old-fashioned intercom by the front door with a little black button you pushed to announce your presence. The speaker looked like it came from the drive-through at Burger King. I pushed the button and a female voice said, "May I help you?"

"I'm here to see Pete Strong."

"Your name?"

"Nicholas Colt."

I stood there and stared stupidly at the speaker while she didn't say anything for a while.

"I'm sorry...do you have an appointment?"

"No."

"Would you like to *make* an appointment?"

"No."

"Sir, Mr. Strong—"

"Just tell him Nicholas Colt is here. Try to tell him before I freeze to death."

A few seconds before my toes needed to be amputated, the deadbolt clicked and the door opened and a slender woman with short brown hair and a beige knit dress ushered me into the reception area. She was a natural beauty with clear blue eyes and a smile that could melt candle wax. She didn't wear any makeup because she didn't need any. She was toned and fit and completely feminine, and only had one fault I could see: the skin around her thumbnails was raw from picking at the cuticles. Otherwise, she was perfect. If I hadn't been a devoted husband and father, I might have asked her to fly to Paris with me.

"Have a seat," she said. "Mr. Strong will be with you shortly."

There was a green leather sofa and a coffee table with some magazines on it. I sat there and learned how to make turkey chili in a Crock-Pot. A FedEx guy brought a package in. Pete's assistant signed for it. The FedEx guy left. Every time the door opened, all the heat in the room got sucked away. I wondered how people managed to live and work under such harsh conditions. They would have to pay me double.

A guy with a long black trench coat and a black cowboy hat came out of Pete's office. He looked sad. Pete opened his office door a couple of minutes later and said, "Come on back, Nicholas."

Pete's desk looked like a budding young landfill. There were a couple of Chinese take-out boxes and several empty Coke cans among the stacks of papers and receipts and general office clutter. Pete lit a cigar. He offered me one and I said no thanks.

"Was that Johnny Cash?" I said.

Pete laughed. "You didn't recognize him?"

"Should I have?"

"He's a country singer. Not as famous as Johnny Cash, but pretty famous."

"I don't know that many country singers. Why would anyone famous be coming to see your crazy ass?"

"Because I am Pete Strong. Private eye to the stars."

"You're a private investigator? Damn, I must have made a wrong turn. I thought this was the VD clinic."

Pete laughed some more. "So what's up, man? How's your case going?"

I told him about my initial confrontation with Lester and Earl. I told him about visiting the Lambs' former residence and then talking to Harvey Mullins, the brother of the man Derek Wahl had shot in the line of duty. I told him about Derek belonging to a church called New Love Ministries. I told him about Allison Parker, the great-niece who was handling the Lambs' estate, and about Virgil Lamb being deep in gambling debt. I told him about Derek Wahl invading my home in Florida and almost killing my wife and daughter.

"Are they OK?" Pete said.

"They're OK. I put them on a plane to the Philippines. I wanted to get them as far from Florida as possible."

"You'd have to leave the planet to get any farther. How is your client taking her brother's death?"

"She said I would pay for it one way or another. I think she's planning to sue me." I told him about my second confrontation with Lester and Earl, about a guy named Bear in a joint called The Bar, and about leaving Lester bleeding in the parking lot at Moe's Ribs.

Pete was scribbling everything down on the back of a hotel receipt. "A lot going on," he said. "You need me to do an extension on your temporary license?"

"I need help," I said. "I need somebody to work with me on this."

Pete laced his hands together and rested his chin on his thumbs. He stared at the wall behind me for thirty seconds or so. "I have two guys who work for me full time, but they're busy as shit right now."

"You could do it yourself."

"I don't think so."

"Come on. It'll be an adventure."

"I don't think so."

"It has to get boring being cooped up in this crummy little office all day."

"You think my office is crummy?"

"Kind of."

He stared at the wall some more. "I'll have to clear it with the boss."

"I thought you were the boss."

"You know the lady you met out front?"

"Your receptionist?"

"She's not my receptionist. She's my wife."

"Oh," I said. "Can I buy y'all some lunch?"

CHAPTER FIFTEEN

Pete's wife, Denise, turned out to be a great conversationalist, as charming and smart as she was physically attractive. She was the kind of person you could talk to all day. The three of us had hamburgers at a place called Ollie's and some apple pie and coffee.

"I need to borrow your husband for a while," I said.

"Borrow him? Ah, just go ahead and keep him." She poked Pete with her elbow.

"I'm serious," I said.

"What's up?"

I told her everything I had told Pete. The deeper I got into it, the graver her expression became.

"I promise I'll take good care of him," I said.

"It sounds too dangerous." She turned to Pete. "Nothing that involves violent criminals and guns and all that, remember? It's what we agreed on when you quit the force and went private. We're doing fine with insurance cases and infidelity and the occasional runaway. We don't need this."

"It's not about the money," Pete said.

"Because I don't have much," I said.

"Then what *is* it about?" She picked at her left thumb with her right index finger.

"It's about the possibility of exposing a nationwide racist organization," Pete said. "And it's about helping a friend. I've decided to do it. Your blessing would be nice."

Pete took a bite of pie.

Denise sipped her coffee.

"You can have him for a week," she said to me. "You hear that, Mr. Strong? One week, and I want you back in the office."

"That's no problem," Pete said. "We have seven days, Mr. Colt. Let's get busy."

—⁂—

Pete and Denise kissed long and hard in the parking lot. They finally said good-bye, and Denise headed back to the office. I drove Pete to his house. He packed a couple of suitcases and threw them into the back of my Jimmy and we headed toward Mont Falcon.

"First thing we need to do is get you out of that motel," Pete said.

"Why?"

"Because Lester and Earl are going to be out for revenge, that's why. Especially Lester. You can't go around ripping people's lips off and expect them to be your buddy next time you see them."

"Those punks don't worry me. Did I tell you I took Lester's knife?" I reached into my pocket, pulled it out, and handed it to Pete. "Genuine stag grips," I said.

"Nice." He slid it into the front pocket of his jeans.

"What are you doing?" I said. "That's mine."

"Not anymore."

"Come on. I stole it fair and square."

"And now I'm stealing it from you."

"Don't make me kick your ass," I said.

Pete laughed. I knew he would give the knife back later, and if he didn't, that would be all right, too.

"So where we going to stay?" I said.

"Friend of mine has a hunting cabin not too far from Black Creek. I called him while I was in the house packing, and he said we could use it for as long as we need it."

"For free?" I said.

"Yep."

"That'll work."

When we got to the motel, I crammed all my gear from the room into the back of the Jimmy and checked out with Beulah at the desk. I asked her about a place called The Bar on Carp Lane. She said she'd never heard of it.

The hunting cabin was only ten minutes away. The dirt road leading to the place ran out and the brush got heavy and we had to park the Jimmy and hike the last hundred yards. The cabin was isolated on a limestone bluff and surrounded by mature hardwoods. It was the perfect base camp for a team of ace detectives. Perfect, except there was no indoor plumbing or electricity or cell phone reception.

"What the fuck?" I said.

"Don't be such a pussy," Pete said. "There's a stack of firewood out back. Why don't you go grab some while I check the kitchen for supplies."

"Why can't I check the kitchen for supplies while *you* go grab some firewood?" I said.

"It's *my* friend's cabin."

"So that makes you the boss?"

"Of course."

"Asshole."

There was a pair of work gloves and a canvas log carrier on the floor near the hearth. I grabbed them and started out the door.

"Watch out for rats," Pete said.

The clouds had brightened and leveled out and it had started to snow. I walked around to the back of the cabin. The woodpile was almost as tall as I was. Someone had done a lot of chopping. I started loading some logs into the carrier. My joints were stiff and my back ached and my ears were ringing from the quiet.

I carried the logs inside. I stacked three of them onto the fireplace grate and found some kindling. Pete came in from the kitchen.

"Can I borrow your lighter?" I said.

He handed it to me. It was a nice cigar lighter. It looked like a miniature blowtorch.

"We're going to need a lot more wood than that to get us through the night," Pete said.

"I'll get more. There's enough wood out there to last until spring. What's in the kitchen?"

"There's a propane stove and utensils and everything. Some canned goods."

"We need to go back to the car and get the coolers," I said.

"It's a long walk. Maybe we could just leave them until tomorrow."

"One of them is full of beer."

"We need to go back to the car and get the coolers," Pete said.

Pete put his coat on and we walked outside. The snow was starting to stick. We got approximately fifty feet from the cabin when a series of gunshots erupted. We instinctively pulled our weapons and dropped to the ground on our bellies. I had Little Bill and Pete had a 9mm Beretta. The ground was cold and covered with crunchy, brown, snow-sugared leaves.

"I thought you said hunting season was over," I said.

"It is."

"Poachers?"

"Or maybe someone shooting at targets."

A bullet whizzed by and thudded into the soil a few feet behind us.

It wasn't someone shooting at targets.

It was someone shooting at us.

A hundred feet or so to the left, I saw a guy in camouflage fatigues come down from a tree. He had a rifle. He ran deeper into the woods and out of sight.

"Are you thinking what I'm thinking?" Pete said.

"Yeah. If someone was trying to kill us, we'd be dead by now."

"You think he was just fucking around?"

"Maybe," I said. "Or maybe it was a poacher posted to guard the territory. Maybe he's off to gather some more guys with more rifles."

I didn't think it was someone trying to scare us off the investigation already, because nobody knew we were out there. Nobody except Pete's wife, Denise, and the guy who owned the cabin.

"We better hurry up and get the beer," Pete said.

"Yeah."

We kept our guns out and walked to the car without further incident. We carried the coolers back to the cabin, sat in the rocking chairs by the fireplace, and popped the tops on a couple of Heinekens. Pete lit a cigar. I didn't like the smell of it, but I didn't say anything. It made me want a cigarette.

"So what's the plan?" Pete said.

"Plan?"

"Yeah, you know, what's on the agenda for this case?"

"I say we drink it."

"Not the beer, dumbfuck."

I laughed. "All right, let's start from the beginning. We need to figure out why someone killed Mrs. Lamb and her daughter-in-law and carved tilted crosses into their foreheads, why Virgil Lamb and Joe Lamb and Derek Wahl disappeared the same day, and why Derek Wahl broke into my house and tried to kill my wife and daughter. We know it wasn't a racial thing, like the plane crash, because so far all the victims have been white. Except for Juliet, of course. She's from the Philippines, but I don't think that was a factor."

"We could start with the obvious," Pete said.

"Which is?"

"That Derek Wahl was responsible for all of it."

"Doesn't add up," I said. "He was on duty that day. He was called to the Lambs' residence for a domestic disturbance. He couldn't have planned that. At first, I thought he'd simply been in the wrong place at the wrong time, that he'd interrupted a loan shark's thugs taking care of business or something. But that theory got shot to hell when he showed up at my house in Florida."

"There's still two people not accounted for," Pete said.

"Virgil Lamb and his grandson Joe," I said. "But Virgil was an old man, in his eighties. It's hard for me to believe he was responsible for all that carnage. I just can't imagine he was physically able."

"That leaves Joe."

"Yeah."

"Maybe Derek Wahl and Virgil Lamb and Joe Lamb were all in cahoots."

"You think Virgil was in on killing his wife and daughter-in-law, and Joe and his mother and grandmother?"

Pete frowned. "Probably not."

"There was someone else at the scene," I said. "The police found DNA from someone other than the Lambs or Derek Wahl. That's who we need to find."

"How do we go about doing that?"

"I don't know. The DNA evidence was a dead end. Didn't show up on any databases. If it had, the cops would probably have somebody in custody by now."

Pete stared into the fire.

I studied the lip of my Heineken can.

"What about that guy named Bear?" Pete said.

"Lester was under quite a bit of stress when he told me about that. He might have made it up. But we'll check into it."

"Want to check into it now?"

"Yeah."

—m—

A winding two-lane skirted by steep rocky cliffs snaked down the western side of the mountain, with only the sharpest curves protected by guardrails. The fact that a blown tire or a momentary lapse in concentration could send us careening a hundred feet to our deaths didn't seem to bother Pete, but I could feel my blood pressure in my eyeballs. I longed for the warmth and flatness of Florida.

"You just passed it," Pete said.

"What?"

"Carp Lane. You just passed it."

"Shit."

A couple of miles and a bucketful of expletives later, I steered my Jimmy onto a dirt path that led into the woods. I waited for a tractor-trailer to lumber by in low gear, and then backed out and turned around.

Carp Lane had been paved, but years and years of harsh winters and neglect had cursed it with uneven cracks and potholes and crumbling edges.

"Should have brought the lunar rover," Pete said.

"They left it on the moon," I said.

"What?"

"They left it up there. I swear. I saw a story about it on TV."

"And we all know everything on TV is true."

"What's your point?" I said.

"It was a hoax. The whole damn thing was a hoax. Nobody ever landed on the fucking moon. All those pictures and videos were taken in the desert. And on soundstages."

"You're crazy. Of course they went to the moon."

"There's a whole lot of evidence to the contrary. And if they left some shit up there, why don't they take some satellite photos now and prove it? I can go to Google Maps and zoom in on my car in my driveway, so why can't they do the same thing with the moon? They don't want to, that's why, because there's nothing there."

"Whatever, man. I've heard all that hoax crap—"

"You passed it."

"What?"

"The Bar. I think that was it back there."

"Shit."

I turned around.

There was a gravel lot on the left side of the building with several parking places and a hitching post for horses. I parked and we got out. The metal roof sloped away from the gables and sheltered a wooden porch cluttered with antique farm equipment and whiskey barrels. Signs advertising products that no longer existed had been tacked to the board-and-batten siding in front.

"There's nobody here," Pete said, cupping his hand against the window and peeking inside.

"I guess we're a little early for happy hour. Or maybe they're only open on certain days."

"We could sit in the truck and wait for a while."

I was about to suggest an alternative plan when a black Dodge Ram pulled into the lot and parked beside my Jimmy. A man got out and walked toward us. It was Ted Grayson. Something about him had changed since the poker game, but I couldn't put my finger on what it was.

"Hey, Nicholas," he said gleefully. "What the hell you up to?"

"Rumor has it a man can get a drink and shoot a game of pool here," I said.

"Now where'd you hear a thing like that?"

"Around."

"Who's your buddy here?"

"I'm sorry. This is Pete Strong. Pete, Ted Grayson."

They shook hands.

"Pleased to meet you," Pete said.

"Likewise."

"Ted owns the meat packing plant," I said. "Grayson's Meats."

"No kidding?" Pete said. "I eat your ham all the time. Good stuff. You can't beat it."

"Well, thank you. We take pride in putting out a quality product."

"Are you saying Ted can't beat his meat?" I said.

They didn't laugh.

"I rode over to check the pilot light on the furnace," Ted said. "It went out the other day, and I wanted to make sure it didn't happen again. You guys are welcome to come in for a spell if you want. I'll even buy you a drink."

"Sounds good," I said. I needed one after traversing that perilous mountain road. Ted opened the door and we walked inside.

CHAPTER SIXTEEN

Ted switched the lights on, revealing what could only be described as a classic roadside honky-tonk. Wood paneling, jukebox, neon beer signs, pickled eggs. There was an L-shaped bar and some booths with globed candles on the tables. Bottles of liquor lined the shelves behind the bar, and a stainless steel beer cooler hummed monotonously in the far left corner.

"I'm assuming you own this place," I said.

"I do," Ted said. "It's illegal as hell, but nobody around here much gives a shit."

"What's back there?" I said, pointing toward a dark archway.

Ted flipped another switch, and the lights came on in the adjacent room. There was one coin-operated pool table and some bistro tables and a big-screen television. Everything was neat and tidy, the ashtrays on tables clean and ready for business.

Ted gestured toward the stools back in the main room. "Have a seat, and I'll be with you in a minute."

Pete and I sat at the bar. We didn't take our coats off.

"I guess this is what they used to call a speakeasy," I said.

"Amazing what you can do with the right kind of money."

"Yeah."

The furnace kicked on.

"How are you planning to approach this?" Pete whispered. "He thinks you're up here scouting fishing locations, right?"

Ted clomped back in before I could answer. He grabbed a bottle of Wild Turkey from the back bar and three glasses. "Bourbon OK?"

Pete nodded.

"Sure," I said.

Ted poured the drinks. "Damn thing went out again. Guess I'm going to have to call someone. You guys know anything about HVAC?"

"I adjusted a thermostat one time," I said.

They didn't laugh again. I was starting to get a complex.

"You still eyeballing spots for the bass rodeo?" Ted said.

"I need to talk to you about that," I said. "I kind of made all that up."

"Huh?"

"I love to fish, but that was never my mission here. I'm a private investigator. Pete and I are working together on a case, the murders at the Lambs' residence a year ago Thanksgiving."

"Well fuck me runnin'. Chris was right about you. He said you were up to something, and damn if he wasn't right."

"He was right, in a way, but I never—"

"So what are you going to do now? Bust me for operating a tavern in a dry county?"

"Not at all. This isn't about you."

"Then what's it about?"

"Ever hear of a Christian militia group called the Harvest Angels?"

"No."

"One of my sources told me a guy named Bear comes in here sometimes. Supposedly he's a member."

"Never heard of him. But I'm not here that much. A couple of bartenders and a bookkeeper mostly run the joint. I pay them under the table, so they're not going to be too happy to be involved in any kind of investigation."

"Maybe you could do me a favor," I said.

"Yeah?"

"Yeah. Just call one of your bartenders and ask him if he knows anything about this Bear fellow."

"You lied to me. Why would I want to help you with anything?"

I thought about telling him I had friends who worked for the IRS, but I was on his turf and didn't want to get into a game of hardball I couldn't win. I decided to come clean all the way.

"I originally thought Virgil Lamb's gambling debts had something to do with his disappearance," I said. "I figured a loan shark sent a couple of guys to the house to take care of business, and that Derek Wahl just happened to show up at the wrong time. The crosses carved into the victims' foreheads initially had me intrigued, because I saw the same thing on a young woman who was killed three years ago. Her name was Leitha Ryan, and she had hired me to find her sister, Brittney, who had run away from home. The man who killed Leitha was an old acquaintance of mine. Later on, I found out he belonged to the religious cult. So at first I thought there might be a connection, and then I dismissed it as paranoia on my part. I couldn't find any evidence to back the assumption. But when Derek Wahl broke into my house—"

"I heard about that. So you're the one who killed Derek?"

"I'm the one. I shot him in the chest."

"He was a good man. Good police officer. He used to come in here and have a drink every now and then."

"I'm sure he was a fine upstanding citizen," I said. "Right up to the time he tried to kill my wife and daughter."

"Something must have happened. That's not the Derek I knew."

"Affiliation with a cult can change a man," I said.

"All right, I understand why you killed Derek, but why the obsession with this Harvest Angels outfit? Why don't you just go on back to Florida and play your music?"

"Because Derek came all the way from Tennessee to invade my home and murder my family. That's pretty goddamn personal. I have to assume I've been targeted. If not by the Harvest Angels, then by someone else. I have to find out who it is and put a stop to it."

"And you want me to help you."

"Well, I did sign those records for you."

Ted reached into his pocket and pulled out his cell phone. A minute later, he penciled a name and address on a cocktail napkin.

Phineas R. Boyle, aka *Bear*.

"Now we're even," Ted said.

CHAPTER SEVENTEEN

Coincidentally, Phineas Boyle's single-wide trailer was located along the same dirt road I had used to turn around on earlier. It was a shabby, depressing little place, with olive green shutters on the windows and a rusted '55 Ford in the yard. A very large pair of jockey shorts trembled on a clothesline stretched between two trees.

"We just going to walk right up to the door and knock?" Pete said.

"Got any better ideas?"

"Maybe we should tail the guy for a while or something. Call me crazy, but white supremacist cults tend to make me nervous."

I pointed toward the underwear. "It's OK. He's already raised the white flag."

"Hillbilly motherfucker."

"I'll go up there and talk to him by myself," I said. "If something bad happens, you can come to my rescue."

"Aren't you just a little bit afraid? You go up there and start confronting this guy—"

"I'm going to act like I'm interested in joining. All I want from this Bear dude is to confirm the existence of a Harvest Angels cell here, and try to find out their location for meetings. Then I'm done. I'll turn it over to the state police and drive on back to Florida."

"Won't he be a tad suspicious about the Negro in your car?"

"That's why I parked this way. He won't be able to see you through the tinted windows."

"This shit makes me nervous."

"We'll be fine. Be back in two shakes."

I got out and walked up to the trailer and knocked on the door. An enormously fat man with long black hair and a full beard answered. It was obvious how he got his nickname.

"Can I help you?"

"Eighty-eight, brother," I said. It was something I learned when I infiltrated the cult called Chain of Light down in Florida three years ago. *H* is the eighth letter of the alphabet. Eighty-eight means double *H*, which stands for *Heil Hitler.*

He smiled. "Eighty-eight," he said. "Come on in."

He stepped aside and allowed me to enter the cramped living room. It was a manly place, with the head of a buck on one wall and three mounted bass on another. He motioned for me to have a seat on a ratty plaid sofa, half of which was covered with dirty laundry. I sat, expecting to sink, but the couch was surprisingly firm. It must not have been in there long enough for Bear's weight to trash the springs. He pulled up a stool that reminded me of a drummer's throne and sat across the coffee table from me.

"Who are you?" he said.

"My name's Nicholas Colt. I'm thinking about moving to the area, and I'm interested in finding some like-minded individuals."

"You believe in taking back the country for the white man?"

"Absolutely."

"You know about the Harvest Angels?"

"That's why I'm here."

"Got some ID?"

I pulled out my wallet and handed him my driver's license. "That picture's a few years old," I said.

"Florida, huh?"

"Yeah."

"Florida's nice, man. Why you want to move to Tennessee?"

"I miss the change of seasons."

"What kind of work you do?"

"I was second ham-boner at a slaughterhouse down in Hallows Cove," I said. "Hoping to get me a job at Grayson's."

A two-liter bottle of Mountain Dew stood greenly erect among the general mishmash of items on the coffee table. Bear picked it up, twisted the cap off, and took a drink. "Want some?"

"No thanks."

"I have some beer in the refrigerator."

"I'm all right."

"There's a meeting here at my house tonight, if you're interested. You can come over and meet some of the guys."

"What time?"

"Around seven. I got plenty of beer. You can bring a bag of chips or something."

"Sounds good. I'll be here."

"Cool, my brother. Well, I got some work to do, you know."

"That's cool. Thanks for the invite. I'm definitely interested."

"See you tonight, then."

I got up and walked toward the door. When I reached for the handle, something hard and unforgiving smashed into the back of my skull.

CHAPTER EIGHTEEN

I woke up with the worst headache of my life. I was positioned in some sort of recliner, maybe a dentist's chair, my arms and legs bound with leather straps. Plastic tubing coiled upward from my left arm to a bag of clear liquid hanging on a pole. My clothes had been stripped off and replaced with a hospital gown. Another plastic tube, a larger one, snaked from between my legs to a bag attached to the foot of the chair. The bag was about half full of what I assumed was my own urine.

A male voice from behind me said, "What's your name?"

"Nicholas Colt," I said.

"Did you sleep well?"

"I don't remember."

"Well, let me assure you, you did."

"Who are you?" I said.

"An old friend, Mr. Colt."

He came around to where I could see him. His features were chiseled and expressionless. I decided to name him Stoneface. I didn't recognize him, but there was something about the voice. Something familiar. I couldn't place it.

"What do you want with me?" I said.

He walked across the room and opened the top drawer on a steel cabinet. He pulled out a small bag of intravenous fluid and a syringe. He uncapped the syringe and injected its contents into a port on the bag. He grabbed a set of tubing and walked back to my chair and piggybacked the new IV into the one on the pole beside me. He opened a clamp, and I watched the fluid drip into a chamber until everything went black.

A period of time lapsed. I didn't know how much. When I opened my eyes, a young woman with blonde hair tied in a bun walked into the room carrying a food tray. She set the tray on a table and wheeled it to my chair and tried to spoon-feed me some green mush from a bowl.

"I don't want that," I said.

She rolled the table back to where it had been and carried the tray out of the room without saying anything. Stoneface came in a few minutes later.

"Why won't you eat?" he said.

"I'm not hungry."

"If you continue to refuse sustenance, I'll be forced to surgically insert a feeding tube into your stomach. Is that what you want?"

I didn't say anything.

"What I'm offering you is a specially formulated paste with precise amounts of protein, carbohydrates, vitamins and minerals, fiber, everything you need to stay healthy. I invented it myself. There's a patent pending. I'm planning to pitch it to NASA one of these days. It doesn't taste bad. I promise."

"I'm not hungry."

"I see. Well, we can't have you starving, so tomorrow I will place a gastrostomy tube into your stomach and we'll feed you that way. I was hoping we could avoid that, but apparently not."

Gastrostomy tube. Why? The last thing I remembered was being in Bear's house, being invited to a meeting of the Harvest Angels. I had to assume Stoneface was a member of the cult, as well. But why in hell would he want to feed me through a tube? Why keep me alive? None of it made any sense.

"Why are you doing this?" I said.

No response.

I wondered what had happened to Pete. Maybe Pete had escaped. Maybe he was out looking for me.

Stoneface got up and walked to the medication cabinet. He did his thing with the small bag of fluid and the vial and syringe. He connected it to my primary drip and a few minutes later, I went reeling into the worst nightmare of my life.

I had an intense hatred for a man I'd never met, and I was out to hurt him in the worst possible way. I knew where he lived. I knew he wasn't home. I took a taxi to his neighborhood and got out a block from his house. I strolled by casually with my hands in my pockets. There was a handkerchief in one front pocket and a small bottle of chloroform in the other, and a ski mask stuffed into one of the back pockets. I kept trying to remember my name but could not. The garage door was open. There was one car parked in there. There was a washer and dryer, and the washer was running. It was on spin cycle. I could hear it whining furiously. I walked up the driveway and into the garage. I crouched down between two large blue Rubbermaid trash cans and put the ski mask on and waited. I pulled the bottle out of my pocket and poured some of the chloroform onto the handkerchief. The washing machine completed its cycle, the basket winding down to a complete stop.

The garage got very quiet, and I had to make sure I didn't make a sound when the woman came out to transfer the clothes from the washer to the dryer. She set the timer and pushed the button and the dryer started humming.

When she opened the door to go back into the house, I came up from behind and pressed the handkerchief soaked with chloroform against her face. The tiniest little whimper escaped from her throat before her muscles went slack and she fell back into my arms. I picked her up and carried her inside and set her on the floor. The girl was sitting at the table eating soup and crackers. She looked at me and screamed. I ran over there and backhanded her in the face. She started crying. Her nose was bleeding. I pressed the handkerchief against her face until she passed out. I found the master bedroom and carried the woman first and then the girl and positioned them side by side on the king-sized bed and took their clothes off. I went back to the kitchen and looked for the knives. I found them in a block on a shelf in the pantry. I pulled one out and felt the edge with my thumb. It was very sharp. I found a roll of duct tape in the drawer under the toaster. I carried the tape and the knife to the master bedroom and bound the girl's wrists and ankles and the woman's and cut the tilted crosses into their foreheads. There was a lot of blood. Deep inside I knew this was wrong, that I was doing a very bad thing, but I couldn't help myself.

I heard something from the direction of the kitchen. Someone had entered the house through the garage. I quickly left the master bedroom and ducked into the smaller bedroom down the hall. The intruder stomped into the master bedroom, and I heard moans and other painful sounds from the woman and the girl. I didn't know what to do. This wasn't part of the script. I gripped the knife and walked back, and there stood The Man I Had An Intense Hatred For. I went at him quickly and viciously with the knife. He dodged the first thrust and I started swiping at him with the blade and I lunged forward like a pirate in a swordfight but The Man I Had An Intense Hatred For spun to the left and the knife went deep into the drywall. By the time I dislodged the knife, he had rolled onto the floor and I went at him overhand knowing this was it and I was going to open him up like a melon but then there was an explosion and another and another and another and the world got hazy and dim and I dropped the knife and fell to the floor. An instant before giving up the ghost, I finally remembered my name. My name was Derek Wahl. My mission had been to kill the family of The Man I Had An Intense Hatred For, but I had failed. A band of demons came for me now and dragged me kicking and screaming all the way to the fiery halls of hell.

I woke up sweating and trembling and gasping for air. It took me a minute to realize my name was Nicholas Colt and that I was not in hell exactly, but strapped to a chair in the workshop of a madman.

Stoneface was sitting at his table across from me, staring me in the eyes, and smiling.

CHAPTER NINETEEN

Trying to find some hope in what appeared to be an utterly hopeless situation, I thought about who might possibly come to my rescue. Juliet and Brittney would be concerned—worried sick was more like it—that I hadn't called them in several days, but they were thousands of miles away in the Philippines. Juliet would undoubtedly try to contact my best friends in Florida, Joe Crawford and Winston "Papa" Fell, to see if they had heard from me. Under normal circumstances, Joe and Papa wouldn't hesitate to jump in a car and drive to Tennessee if they thought I was in trouble. But Papa was still recovering from his gallbladder surgery, which hadn't gone well and was probably going to end up in malpractice litigation, and Joe was in Denmark schmoozing some wealthy brewery owners who had expressed interest in Florida real estate. Joe would postpone his business meetings and fly back to the States in a heartbeat if he thought the situation warranted it, but even if he did come looking, the odds of him actually finding me were astronomical. I was the proverbial needle in a haystack. *I* didn't even know where I was. The only ally who might have had a clue was Pete Strong, but I had a feeling he was being held captive, as well. He would have sent in the cavalry already if he'd been able.

So there was no one. There was only me, and I was helpless.

I had no way of knowing if it was day or night when Stoneface and a female assistant wheeled a stainless steel cart in and parked it next to my chair. They were both wearing surgical masks and gowns. On top of the cart there were a variety of syringes and medication vials and shiny instruments spread out over a blue towel. There was a white tube about eight inches long and about the caliber of a drinking straw with ports on one end and what looked like a deflated balloon on the other.

"What's your name?" Stoneface said.

"Nicholas Colt. I already told you that."

"I'm going to insert your G-tube now. This is what you get for refusing to eat."

"I want regular food," I said. "Not that green goop."

"You can't have regular food."

"Why not?"

"Because I said so."

The assistant lifted my gown and swabbed my belly with iodine. She draped me with blue towels, leaving a naked rectangle under my left ribcage. Stoneface unwrapped a pair of sterile gloves and put them on his hands. The assistant did likewise. He held his right palm out flat and she slapped a scalpel into it and he moved toward me focusing on the windowed area on my abdomen. The crazy son of a bitch was going to cut me, and there wasn't a damn thing I could do about it.

"You're fucking insane," I said.

"I was going to give you some anesthetic, but I've decided against it. The incision will be very small, and after a few hours, the excruciating pain will subside. Tomorrow, I can start pumping a product called Jevity into your gut and your refusal to accept sustenance will no longer be an issue."

The overhead light glinted on the scalpel's blade, creating a star effect through my teary eyes. Stoneface bent over me, holding the knife like a pencil with his right hand and pulling the skin on my belly taut with his left.

"Stop," I shouted. "All right. You win. I'll eat your goddamn predigested slop. Just don't cut me."

When I was twelve, I got into a fight with my stepfather and he ended up stabbing me with a steak knife. My relationship with cutlery has been a little strained ever since. To say I hate knives is an understatement.

"You've wasted enough of my time," Stoneface said. "I should have done this in the first place."

"Please. I swear to God, I'll do whatever you want me to do."

He came closer with the blade. I started bucking and thrashing and twisting in my seat.

"Be still, or you'll be sorry."

"Fuck you!" I spit in his face. The assistant wiped him off with a towel. He set the scalpel down and left the room and came back with another cart. This one had a car battery on it and a black metal box the size of a dictionary. The box had a toggle switch on the front and a dial that looked like the volume control to an amplifier. A set of wires connected the battery terminals to one side of the box, and another set of wires with alligator clips on the ends coiled out from the other side. Stoneface grabbed the alligator clips and attached them to my scrotum. He turned the dial to 2 and flipped the switch. My body stiffened and a million buzzing acid-dipped hornets jammed their stingers into my testicles. Boiling hot seltzer coursed through my veins in waves. My jaw dropped and my eyes bulged and a long guttural howl erupted from somewhere deep in my chest.

Then it was over. Stoneface cut the juice, but my balls still felt as though someone had danced on them with baseball cleats. The assistant wiped the drool from my chin and neck with a piece of gauze.

"Shall we crank it up to three?" Stoneface said.

I couldn't speak. I shook my head and grunted like a caveman.

"Are you going to be still now?"

I nodded. I still couldn't figure out why Stoneface wanted to keep me alive with a feeding tube. Just to torture me some more? Some kind of revenge for killing Derek Wahl? Was it because I shut down the Harvest Angels in Florida three years ago?

I closed my eyes, and a few minutes later, I felt the cold blade slice into my skin.

CHAPTER TWENTY

I woke up alone. My stomach hurt where Stoneface had inserted the gastrostomy tube. He hadn't started the feeding yet. I was very hungry. It had been days since I had eaten. There was a pillow under my head, and someone had been kind enough to cover me with a blanket. I would have given a million dollars for a pint of bourbon and a hamburger and some French fries.

The door opened and in walked Stoneface with a plastic bottle full of liquid the color of chocolate milk. He had some clear plastic tubing and an electric pump that controlled the feeding rate. I had interviewed a patient in a nursing home one time and recognized the setup.

"What's your name?" he said.

"Nicholas Colt. Something wrong with your memory?"

"I trust you slept well."

"My ass is sore from sitting in this chair and there's a gnawing pain in my gut where you cut me open. Yeah, I slept like a fucking baby."

He clamped the pump onto my IV pole. He spiked the bottle and then fed the tubing through a chamber and turned the pump on and primed it. There was a large syringe and a plastic beaker half full of water on the table beside my chair. He drew some water into the syringe and lifted my gown and flushed the tube going into my stomach. The water sent a chill through me. He connected the tubing from the pump to the tube going into my stomach and set the rate on the pump's little computer and started mainlining the formula into my body. I felt twinges of pain but nothing unbearable. Then I felt a cramp in my lower abdomen.

"I need to go to the bathroom," I said.

"You need to have a bowel movement?"

"Yes."

He left the room. Two muscular guys with pistols on their hips came in and unbuckled my straps. They helped me into a clean gown. They handcuffed me and led me down a hallway with my IV pole and urinary drainage bag in tow. We stopped at a narrow wooden door.

"You got five minutes," one of the guys said.

I walked into the bathroom and shut the door. I had no idea what time it was, or even what day, but there was a window with frosted glass in there, and it looked to be bright and sunny outside.

Outside was where I wanted to be.

I crouched beside the toilet, nearly losing my balance, and sat on my hands. I rocked onto my back, folded my knees, fed my feet through the loop one at a time.

Now my hands were in front.

I stood on the IV tubing and yanked the needle out of my vein. It bled some, but not bad. There was a buff-colored tube coming out of my urethra. It led to a larger clear plastic tube, and I managed to twist and separate the two where they joined. I unhooked the tubing from the feeding pump and left it dripping on the floor. I capped the tube going into my stomach with the little stopper that was conveniently attached to the end.

I looked at the window. It was an old aluminum frame and I knew it would squeak when I tried to raise it. I gently opened the cabinet under the sink, saw an assortment of cleaning solvents, deodorizers, brushes, and sponges. There was a bottle of white shoe polish and a rusty pipe wrench. I scanned for something to lubricate the window tracks with, but Stoneface must have kept the WD-40 and the petroleum jelly in other locations.

There was a bar of soap on the vanity. I picked it up and smelled it. Ivory. I climbed into the bathtub, gripped the soap firmly with both cuffed hands, and slid it up and down the window tracks. I dipped my hands into the toilet bowl and then dribbled some water onto the tracks. Now they were wet and slippery. I turned the lock lever, freeing the bottom half of the window, and then pressed forward and upward at the same time. In a few seconds, the window was completely open. I stood on the lip of the tub, reached with my arms, hooked my elbows on the outside of the window frame, and hoisted myself through. Now I was half in, half out. I shifted my weight and tumbled headfirst to the frosty ground six feet below.

I did a somersault, and in one fluid motion rose to my feet and took off running. I was barefoot, completely naked except for the hospital gown. It was freezing. I guessed it to be in the midtwenties, but the adrenaline pumping through my veins kept me from feeling it. There was a tree line a hundred feet or so from the house. I ran for it. It was my goal to make it there and disappear into the woods. There was a barbed wire fence guarding the perimeter of the property, the kind with three strands you see on cattle ranches, but I figured there was enough room for me to crawl under it. I ran, fast as I could, my breath coming out in white puffs.

I was probably about halfway from the house to the woods when a voice from behind me shouted, "Stop, or I'll shoot!" I started zigzagging, knowing it would be a miracle for them to hit anything from that distance with handguns. I didn't figure they would shoot me, anyway. Stoneface wanted me alive. He wanted to make me as miserable as possible for as long as possible. He wanted to use me for his demented experiments. Why, I didn't know. But he was going to be pissed when he found out those goons had allowed his prized lab rat to escape. They wouldn't shoot me. I was counting on it. I was counting on it right up to the time I heard the *rat-a-tat-tat* of automatic rifle fire. I kept zigzagging. Blood started trickling out of the hole in my left arm where the IV had been. It was coming out in a steady stream and leaving a trail of droplets on the ground. My hands were cuffed and I couldn't reach the wound to put pressure on it. It wouldn't be hard for them to track me, with or without dogs. I tried not to think about it. I kept running.

I was almost to the fence. I glanced over my shoulder and saw Stoneface's muscle heads running toward me. I didn't have time to get down on the ground and try to scoot under the bottom strand of barbed wire. My only chance was to hurdle it. I estimated the top strand to be about three and a half feet from the ground. It had been a long time since I'd done any jumping. My lungs were on fire and my legs felt like rubber. My heart was about to explode.

The hospital gown was going to be a problem. I was afraid it was going to get snagged on the barbed wire. I reached behind my head and pulled the slipknot on the tie string. The sleeves were held together with snaps and I jerked them loose and the garment floated away in my wake. Now I was naked and it was twenty-something degrees and I knew I was probably going to die soon.

In eighth grade, there was a high jump set up in the gym, and we learned several different techniques to clear the bar. One of them was called the Fosbury Flop. You turned and launched yourself backward, arching your back at precisely the right moment and landing on your shoulders on a padded mat on the other side. My personal record using the Fosbury Flop was five feet, four inches. It was a height any serious track and field athlete would laugh at, and it was thirty-some years ago last time I tried it. I decided it was my best shot. I decided to go for it. The skin on my back would either be shredded by barbed wire or I would end up a quadriplegic from the landing or I would make it to the other side OK and gallop into the woods. Assuming Stoneface's men didn't lose their patience and open up with the machine guns.

Everything started moving in slow motion as I approached the fence. I decided to aim for a pile of leaves and pine needles that had blown between two of the posts, thinking it might cushion my fall. I ran toward the fence line at an angle and started making my turn about ten feet from the spot where I planned to leap. I was a couple of feet away now with my back to the fence and my eyes on the men chasing me and I went airborne and arched my back and easily cleared the top strand of wire, but the urinary catheter dangling from between my legs got caught on a barb and something big got yanked from my bladder and down through my urethra and I fell and rolled on the ground on the other side of the fence feeling as though I'd given birth to a cantaloupe.

All those hours in the gym worked against Stoneface's men now as they tried to squeeze their enormous chests and shoulders and arms under the bottom strand of barbed wire. I got up and ran into the forest. There was no trail. The dead and prickly underbrush was probably doing a number on my feet, but they were numb from the cold. I couldn't feel them at all. It was if they weren't there. The inside of my penis, on the other hand, felt as though it had been scoured with a brush.

I ran deeper and deeper into the woods, changing directions every few seconds, intentionally finding fallen trees and other obstacles that might slow the hounds I figured would eventually be tracking me.

I came upon a clearing and stopped and gazed up at one of the most horrific things I'd ever seen.

Swinging in the breeze from the largest branch of an old oak tree was my dear friend Pete Strong.

Pete was dead. They had hanged him.

CHAPTER TWENTY-ONE

I didn't have time to grieve. I was going to die of hypothermia if I didn't do something fast.

Pete's feet were only about twelve inches from the ground. I patted his pockets and found Lester's knife, a wallet, a set of keys, and the butane lighter he used for cigars. I cut the rope binding his wrists. I unzipped his coat and pulled it off him and wrapped it around my shoulders. His holster was still on his belt but the 9mm Beretta was gone. I untied his boots and pulled them and a nice pair of thermal socks off his feet. It was clumsy and cumbersome working with the handcuffs on, but I managed to pull his pants off next and his long underwear. I unbuttoned his shirt and pulled that off. Now he was naked except for a T-shirt and a pair of boxers and a gold Rolex. I took the watch. It was a little loose on my wrist, but not loose enough to fall off.

I put the long johns and the pants on, then the socks and boots. It was impossible to put the shirt on, so I held it to my chest to cover the bare spot and headed deeper into the woods.

I needed to find a road, but I had no idea which way to go. Daylight was fading fast. I would be harder to find in the dark, but the temperature would plummet overnight and I would probably freeze to death before morning. My only hope was to find some sort of shelter and build a fire.

I stopped and listened. Leaves crunched and twigs snapped under the heavy footsteps of Stoneface's men. They were in the woods. I could hear them talking.

"I'll be damned. He stripped the motherfucker."

"Yeah. Blood trail's gone and it's getting dark. Let's go back. We'll never find him out here."

"We have to find him. We're going to have our elbows broken with a sledgehammer if we don't find him. You know what it's like to not be able to feed yourself or wipe your own ass?"

"Let's at least go get some flashlights."

A pause, and then, "You go. I'll wait here in case he doubles back."

"All right."

The one going for the flashlights faded away at a trot. The other one waited at the site where they'd hanged my friend. I decided to do what he wanted. I decided to double back.

I took the boots off, tied the laces together, and carried them around my neck. I crept through the woods in stocking feet, making as little noise as possible. By the time I got back to where Pete had been executed, Muscle Head Number One had a campfire going. He sat in front of it, warming his hands. He looked comfy-cozy. I snuck up behind him and violently jerked the handcuff chain around his throat. He struggled for about five seconds, and then I felt his trachea cave in. I let go, expecting to hear a gasp or two, but he never took another breath.

I searched his pockets, but Muscle Head Number Two must have been carrying the key to the cuffs. Number One had a wallet and a comb and a Ford ignition key and a half-eaten protein bar. I took all of it and his pistol and walkie-talkie, and hid behind a cedar tree and waited. I put my boots back on. I gobbled the chocolate in three bites. It tasted like a stale brownie laced with vitamins. Not something I normally would have chosen, but under the circumstances it was like tiramisu at the Ritz.

I wondered if Number Two would bring a search team when he returned. I doubted it. He was probably too embarrassed to admit that he and his newly deceased friend had allowed me to escape. The human ego is a powerful force. World leaders invade countries because of it. Otherwise intelligent people will go to great measures to avoid having it bruised, and I had the feeling Muscle Head Number Two wasn't exactly Einstein in the first place.

Pete's Rolex had a little button you could push to make the face light up.

Five forty.

Twilight.

The embers from Number One's fire cast an orange glow on his corpse and the surrounding area. The warmth of it beckoned like a Siren, but I wanted to maintain an element of surprise so I stayed where I was and tried to keep my teeth from chattering.

Number Two crunched in carrying a flashlight and a small cooler. An Uzi hung from a strap around his neck. I was right. He didn't bring anyone with him. He ran to his fallen comrade and said, *Oh shit,* and knelt beside him.

He tried to shake him awake. "Kevin. Kevin!"

I stepped out and aimed the pistol at Number Two's chest.

"Kevin's not with us anymore," I said.

He looked up at me. "Son of a bitch."

"You got that right. I want you to grab your weapon by the barrel, pull it off your neck, and toss it this way. Deviate from those instructions and I'll put a hole in your heart."

He grabbed his weapon by the barrel, pulled it off his neck, and tossed it toward me.

"You going to kill me?" he said.

"Maybe not. Depends on how well you cooperate. You got the key to these handcuffs?"

"Yes."

"Where is it?"

"In my pocket."

"Which pocket?"

"It's in the right front pocket of my pants."

"You got another gun?"

"No."

"I want you to reach into the right front pocket of your pants, pull out the key to the handcuffs, set the key on top of the cooler, and take five steps backward. Deviate from those instructions and I'll put a hole in your heart."

He reached into the right front pocket of his pants, pulled out the key to the handcuffs, set the key on top of the cooler, and took five steps backward. I walked to the cooler and picked up the key and managed to free myself by the dying light of Kevin's campfire.

"What's your name?" I said.

"Koby."

"Like the cheese?"

"Like Toby with a K."

"You H-A?"

"What's that?"

"Don't play dumber than you are."

"I don't know what you're talking about," he said.

"I think you know damn well what I'm talking about. I'm talking about a Christian militia group called the Harvest Angels. Along with a slew of other terrorist acts, they were responsible for a plane crash twenty-some years ago that killed my wife and daughter and all the members of my band. My wife was from Jamaica. It was a racial thing. Now I don't want to jump to any conclusions or anything, but my friend dangling from the tree branch here is also a person of color. Maybe that's just a coincidence. And maybe, just maybe, it was a coincidence that I got clobbered over the head by a guy named Bear—who I know for a fact is a member of the Harvest Angels—and magically ended up in that little house of horrors with Dr. Stoneface and you and Kevin and the rest of the brainwashed bunch. What do you think, Toby with a K? Was all that just a coincidence?"

"I still don't know what you're talking about."

He wasn't going to talk unless I made him talk. I decided to make him talk.

"I'm going to put these cuffs on you," I said. "I want you to turn around, slowly, and put your hands behind your back. Deviate from those instructions and I'll—"

He ran up and kicked the glowing embers like a field goal. A fountain of orange exploded in my face, the sparks searing my skin like acid-dipped needles. My left eye felt as though someone had stabbed it with a soldering iron. Toby with a K was quicker than he looked. He was on me in an instant. He tackled me and we fell together into the cedar tree I'd been hiding behind earlier. The Uzi was still on the ground. I had a grip on the pistol, but he had a grip on my wrists and he had eaten more PowerBars than I had. He had me pinned to the ground with those gorilla meat hooks of his, and the situation seemed hopeless until he got down close to my face and said, "You're going to die, bitch." That was a big mistake. I thrust my head forward and clamped down on his nose like a pit bull. I directed every ounce of my rapidly diminishing energy to my jaw muscles, slicing through the tough cartilage with the sharp edges of my incisors. I bit his nose completely off and spit it back at him. He rose with a gurgling scream, his hands pressed against his ruined face trying to stop the blood from gushing. I stood and took aim and blasted a hole the size of a quarter through his breastplate. The bullet exited through his back, a splatter of blood and flesh landing on the hot coals with a sizzle.

"Dumbfuck," I said. "I warned your ass."

CHAPTER TWENTY-TWO

The gunshot reverberated through the mountain like a thunderbolt, and I knew it wouldn't be long before Kevin and Koby and I were missed. It wouldn't be long before a posse was sent out to find us. I put Pete's shirt and coat on, and I pulled Koby's wool skullcap off his head and put it on mine. I slung the Uzi around my neck, grabbed the flashlight and the cooler, and headed west. I wanted to get as far from Stoneface's compound as possible. With a little luck, I would find a road and hitch a ride and alert the authorities, and this whole ordeal would be over before daylight.

I hiked for about an hour and then decided to stop and check out the cooler. There were two peanut butter and jelly sandwiches and some more PowerBars and four bottles of spring water and another flashlight. I opened one of the bottles and swallowed half the water in a single gulp. I unwrapped one of the sandwiches and ate it, trudging through the dead underbrush as fast as my weakened legs would carry me. It was 7:30. I was missing *Jeopardy*. Funny, the things that go through your mind in dire situations sometimes. About ten minutes later, the walkie-talkie squawked.

"K-One, do you copy?"

Rule #9 in Nicholas Colt's *Philosophy of Life*: Nobody ever got into any trouble by just shutting the fuck up. But I don't always follow my own rules. I keyed the TALK button. "This is Nicholas Colt," I said. "Who am I talking to?"

"Where are Kevin and Koby?"

It was Stoneface. I recognized his voice now. I put the cooler down and sat on it. "Did you hear the gunshot a while ago, around five forty-five?"

"No."

"I see. Well, the shot you didn't hear sent a bullet tearing through dear old Koby's chest. Before that, I strangled Kevin to death with a handcuff chain. Both your boys are dead."

"You'll never make it off this mountain alive, Colt."

I almost laughed. He sounded like he was reading from the script of an old TV show, *The Lone Ranger* or something.

"Fuck you," I said. "I will leave this mountain alive, and you're going to leave it in the back of a police car. I shut you motherfuckers down in Florida, and I'm going to shut your asses down here."

"You don't know what you're talking about," he said.

"What happened to Virgil Lamb and his grandson Joe? They buried somewhere on your property? Or maybe they're part of your little cult, like Derek Wahl was."

I heard a click, and then silence. I got up and continued walking. It was cold, but I was deep in the forest and there wasn't any wind. It was practically comfortable with the clothes I had on. Every twenty minutes or so I stopped and took a drink of water and nibbled on a PowerBar for energy.

I made it to a ridge with a recess that might have been considered a cave. It was only about ten feet deep, but it felt twenty degrees warmer inside. I cleared an area at the mouth and arranged some chunks of limestone in a circle and started a fire with twigs and some branches from a fallen oak. I was exhausted. I decided to stay there and rest for a couple of hours. I planned to go back out at midnight and carry on in the same direction and continue looking for a road.

A small clearing around the ridge allowed light to shine in from the moon and stars. I stood at the edge of the cliff and breathed the sweet cold air in deeply. The fire crackled and the heat from it stabbed some circulation back into my feet. After a few minutes, I crawled into the deepest part of the cave and leaned against the back wall. I pulled the collar of Pete's coat over my nose and mouth, closed my eyes, and fell asleep.

In my dream, I was eleven years old. I sat on a bench outside the Hollows Cove Mortgage and Trust Company, chewing on a stick of licorice, waiting for my stepfather to take care of some business inside. A man on the corner opposite the bank stood beside a big hand-painted sign that said NOOSES ON SALE. Not *for* sale, but *on* sale, as if you needed to hurry on over to get one cheap. I rose from my seat and crossed the intersection.

There were several lengths of rope lying on the ground, each with a hangman's knot on one end. I counted the loops on a couple of the knots and, sure enough, there were thirteen, just as I'd always heard.

"What are the ropes for, mister?"

"They're for ugly redhead retards who jaywalk."

"I ain't no retard. And it ain't no crime to have red hair."

"But jaywalking *is* a crime. Haven't you heard the news? It's a hanging offense now."

"You're funny, mister."

My stepfather appeared then, seeming to be in a foul humor, the way he got when he drank too much whiskey the night before.

He grabbed me by the arm. "What do you think you're doing?"

"Just talking to the noose salesman here."

"I'll take one of those," my stepfather said to the man.

"Buy one, get one half-price. While they last."

"I'll just be needing the one."

My stepfather handed the man some money and picked out a length of rope, checking the knot to make sure it functioned properly.

"Why'd you buy that noose?" I asked on the ride home, but my stepfather didn't answer.

And we didn't go home.

He steered the truck through an open gate and parked beside a tobacco barn. He got out, grabbed the rope with one hand and my hair with the other, and pulled me shouting and screaming to the inside of the barn. Next thing I knew I was standing on a rickety stool with my hands tied with baling twine, the loose end of the rope secured to a roof beam and the business end to my neck. It was hot in the barn, probably over a hundred degrees, and the noose was tight and the hemp coarse and I could feel it burning into my sweaty skin. I teetered on the stool, knowing a loss of balance meant instant death.

"Why are you doing this?"

"You heard the man. Jaywalking's a hanging offense these days. Nothing I can do about that."

"Please, I'll be good. I promise."

"You should have thought of that before. Too late now."

A wasp flew overhead. I followed it to its nest with my eyes.

"May as well get rid of them damn things while I'm at it," my stepfather said. He picked up a can of gasoline, screwed the lid off, sprinkled some in the straw around the stool, and then doused my pants with the rest.

He lit a match.

Now I had a choice. I could jump off the stool and hang myself, or I could stand there and burn. Up to this point, I'd thought all this was just another one of my stepfather's ways to scare some sense into me but those gasoline fumes were real and making me dizzy and the flame on the end of that match was real and the noose and the rickety stool and the wasp's nest, and it was hot, hot, hot in the barn; and just when I thought, *This is it, I'm going to die now*, I woke with my heart hammering in my ears and sweat dripping from my forehead.

I scooted back toward the mouth of the cave, stood and stretched. I scooped some dirt onto my little fire pit and extinguished the lingering coals.

I looked down into the ravine and saw a dozen or so pinpoints of light heading my way. The posse hadn't waited for daylight. They were coming for me now. How the hell they were tracking me in the dark I didn't know. I opened the cooler and grabbed the fresh flashlight and a bottle of water and started climbing the ridge as fast as I could.

CHAPTER TWENTY-THREE

I figured they were ten, maybe fifteen minutes behind me. I was deep in the forest again, moving as swiftly as possible while trying to avoid a million eye-gouging tree branches. The icy mountain air seared my lungs and throat and the sound of my heartbeat pounded through my jawbone like a jackhammer. I tripped and fell and thought about staying down. I thought about staying down and blowing my own brains out, but I wanted to see Juliet and Brittney again. They were my driving force. They were what I lived for. I wanted to see them again, but my legs felt like rubber and when I tried to stand, they buckled under my weight. I couldn't walk. I couldn't take another step. I inched along on my elbows, knowing Stoneface and his henchmen would catch up soon. They would catch up soon, but I still had the pistol and the Uzi and I wasn't about to go down without a fight.

I switched the flashlight off and waited in the still blackness. In the distance, I heard someone playing an old gospel song called "Til the Storm Passes By" on a harmonica. I shook my head, but the lonesome wail persisted. When I finally realized it wasn't an auditory hallucination, I crawled toward the sound and came upon a clearing and a shack that had been built into the side of the hill. Smoke rose from a galvanized steel pipe in the roof and candlelight glowed dimly from the single window in front. I hid the Uzi behind a bush. I doubted the occupant would be very happy if he or she looked out and saw me standing there with a machine gun. I kept the pistol tucked in my waistband. Somehow I found the strength to stand then and I staggered to the door and banged on it frantically. A short chubby man with a long white beard and a .44 Magnum answered.

Santa Claus meets Dirty Harry.

"What do you want?" he said.

"I'm being followed. They're going to kill me."

"Who's going to kill you?"

"I don't have time to explain. Please, help me."

He tugged on his beard with one hand and held the .44 pointed toward the ground with the other.

"You're out of your mind," he said. "Get away from my house."

I drew my pistol and aimed it directly between his eyes. He twitched, started to raise the .44, and then thought better of it.

"Drop the gun," I said.

He dropped it. "What do you want with me, mister?"

"Take three steps backward," I said.

He took three steps backward and I knelt down and picked up the revolver, never taking my eyes off him. The .44 was a hulk of a weapon, heavy and black and unwieldy. I didn't want to carry it around, so I whizzed it toward the bush where I'd hidden the Uzi. It landed with a thud. I kept the pistol aimed at Dirty Santa and stepped inside and closed the door.

The cabin was one room. There was a fireplace and a table with two chairs and a twin-size bed and a ratty old recliner. No electricity, no indoor plumbing. Something in a cast iron pot over the fire smelled wonderful.

"They'll be here in a few minutes," I said. "I don't know how they're tracking me in the dark, but they are. I need to hide somewhere, and I need for you to tell them you haven't seen me."

"Why should I help you?"

"Because if you don't, I'm going to shoot your ass."

"Good enough reason, I reckon. The only place to hide is under the bed."

"All right."

I walked to the bed, got down on the floor and scooted underneath it. I scooted all the way against the wall. There was a sliver of vision between the floor and the quilt and when the knock came, I saw the old man's bare feet flap across the pine boards to answer the door.

"Can I help you?" Santa said.

"We're looking for a very dangerous man."

"Are you the police?"

"Just some concerned citizens. We think this very dangerous man might have come this way. Has anybody been by here this evening?"

"Nobody ever comes by here," Santa said. "And that's the way I like it."

"I see. I'm going to leave you one of our walkie-talkies. If you happen to see a man about six feet tall with sandy blond hair and beard, give us a call."

"I'll sure do it."

Santa closed the door and several sets of footsteps clomped off the porch. I waited a few minutes and then wriggled out from beneath the bed.

"You did good," I said. "Thank you."

He sat at the table, reached into his pocket and pulled out a Ziploc bag with an ounce or so of marijuana in it and a pack of rolling papers. "Mind telling me what this is all about?"

I walked to the table and sat in the chair across from him. I told him what this was all about while he pinched some of the weed from the bag and expertly constructed a joint the size of a roll of dimes. He lit the fatty, took two tokes, and then passed it my way.

I took a hit.

It would have been rude not to.

It was the first time in three years I'd drawn smoke of any kind into my lungs. It was sweet and smooth and a happy calm washed over me almost immediately.

"Thanks," I said. "I needed that."

"What's your name?"

"Nicholas Colt."

"Dempsey Waters. Pleased to meet you."

"Likewise. Look, I need to find a road and a ride and get the hell out of here."

"I can point you toward the road. You want a bite to eat first?"

I hesitated for a second and then accepted his offer for food. He ladled some of the stew from the cast iron pot into bowls and brought the bowls to the table. He opened a cupboard, tore open a package of flour tortillas, stacked some on a plate. He brought those and some salt and pepper in shakers that had probably been stolen from a lunch counter.

"What is this?" I said.

"Just some venison with taters and onions."

"It's marvelous."

"I'm kindly partial to it myself. Mind if I ask you a personal question?"

I shook some black pepper onto my stew. "You can ask," I said.

"Why'd you come down here and start messing with these guys in the first place?"

I told him about the plane crash in 1989. When I got to the part about the Harvest Angels being responsible, someone started pounding on the door.

CHAPTER TWENTY-FOUR

I hurried back under the bed.

Dempsey answered the door. A man stepped inside holding the .44 I'd slung toward the bush and the Uzi I'd hidden under it.

"This your handgun?" the man said.

"Never seen it before."

The man raised the revolver, cocked the hammer back, and shot Dempsey point-blank in the chest. Dempsey collapsed like a marionette with its strings cut.

The man fired toward the bed. The slug opened a smoking hole the size of a quarter in one of the pine boards in front of me, just inches from my face.

"Come on out, Colt."

I squeezed off several rounds from beneath the bed, and one of them found its mark. A flower of dark red blood bloomed from the man's left kneecap. He said *fuck* and fell to the floor on top of Dempsey. I scooted out, stood, and finished him with one to the head.

I looked out the window, saw only blackness, but I figured the rest of the posse was somewhere nearby and would be drawn by the gunfire. I took the Uzi from the dead man and walked out. There was a stack of firewood off to one side of the house and something under a large sheet of woven nylon. I pulled the tarp off and to my amazement found a Kawasaki four-wheeler parked there and a metal gas can. I should have known. It would have been very hard for Dempsey to live so deeply in the woods with no means of transportation. I climbed aboard and reached for the ignition switch, but the key wasn't there. I ran back inside and searched the pockets of Dempsey's pants and coat, no luck. I opened every drawer and cabinet, fingered the recesses in the recliner, scanned the walls for a nail or a hook. I even sifted through Dempsey's bag of pot, but the key was nowhere to be found.

I gave up on it. As I stepped over the corpses and walked through the threshold, I heard footsteps approaching through the dry and frozen underbrush. More than one set. I swept the area with machine gun fire, kept shooting until the Uzi was out of ammo.

Silence. The bursts from the automatic weapon had either rendered me completely deaf or the bad guys completely dead. Since nobody returned fire, I figured the latter.

The Uzi was useless to me now. I tossed it into the house. I looked down at Dempsey and said good-bye. He had helped me. He had been kind to me, and had paid the ultimate price. As I stared into his lifeless eyes, I noticed the tiny metallic beads around his neck glinting in the firelight. I bent down and pulled the chain from beneath his shirt. His skin was as cold as raw liver. On the end of the necklace was a set of dog tags and a small key. I jerked the chain and it broke. I took the key and left the tags on his bloody chest.

I ran out to the four-wheeler, climbed on, and jammed the key into the ignition. Nothing. The damn thing wouldn't start. The battery was dead. I got off and checked the cables. Dempsey had disconnected them. I twisted the terminals onto the posts and tried the ignition again and the engine roared to life. I switched the headlight on and sped into the woods.

I didn't know if I'd killed all the men in Stoneface's posse with the Uzi. Probably not. They had probably scattered. It would have been stupid for them to stay in a cluster. The pistol in my waistband had a twelve-round magazine, and I'd already spent half of those killing the man who killed Dempsey. That left me with six rounds to fend off an indeterminate number of creeps.

I wasn't feeling real good about my chances.

I'd left the .44 Magnum in the house, thinking it too cumbersome to carry around. That was my rationale, but that was before I had wheels. Now I wished I had brought the extra firepower. Leaving the revolver was a mistake. My mind was foggy from fatigue and marijuana and I had made a huge mistake, one that could possibly cost me my life.

I motored through the brush in no particular direction. The four-wheeler's engine was loud and the headlight was on, making me an easy target. I kept expecting to feel a bullet tear into my back, but it didn't happen. I must have chosen the right path. I must have gotten lucky for once.

I rode for about thirty minutes and stopped when I came to a strip of gravel just wide enough for one vehicle. I wanted to follow it, but I wasn't sure which way to go. Left or right? One way probably led to a residence, the other to a road. I wanted the road. Stoneface's posse would be checking all the houses in the area, same as they had checked Dempsey's, and I didn't want to get into a similar situation elsewhere. I didn't want to get anyone else killed.

I chose left, pegged the throttle, and a few minutes later saw lights through the window of another cabin. I turned around, hoping nobody in the house had heard the four-wheeler's engine.

Now I was on the way to a road for sure. I was on the brink of victory. This nightmare was almost over. I could feel it.

I made it to the two-lane blacktop and again had to choose a direction. I turned right. I wound through the gears, pushing the son of a bitch for all it was worth. It was bitter cold. The speedometer said forty-five, but the stinging needles piercing my face made it feel like eighty. I squinted my eyes into narrow slits, the tears sweeping across my temples and drying to a salty crust almost immediately. My vision was blurred and my lungs were on fire and every joint in my body felt as though someone had pounded it with a hammer. None of that mattered. I was on my way back to the world. I was on my way to freedom.

Then I heard a siren behind me. I looked back and saw blue lights flashing and within seconds, the cruiser was inches from my tail. I slowed down, veered to the shoulder, braked to a stop.

Through a loudspeaker the officer said, "Put your hands behind your head with your fingers laced together."

I did. He came from behind and slapped some handcuffs on me and then walked around to where I could see him. It was a state trooper. I tried to blink him into focus, to no avail. The combination of cold wind and sleep deprivation had done a number on my eyes. I couldn't have fingered him in a lineup if my life depended on it.

"I can explain," I said.

"Stand up."

I dismounted the four-wheeler, losing my balance so badly I nearly fell. He frisked me and found the 9mm tucked in my waistband.

"Like I said, I—"

"Shut up."

He gripped the back of my neck with one hand and the cuffs with the other and shoved me toward the police car.

"Am I under arrest?"

"Shut up."

"Aren't you supposed to read me my rights and shit?"

"Shut the fuck up."

He opened the back door and guided me into the seat. I didn't resist. It was comfortably warm inside the car. I knew it was only a matter of time before someone would listen to my story. When they realized that I was the good guy, and that there were a whole bunch of bad guys back at the ranch, I would be on my way to Florida and Stoneface and crew would be on their way to the Tennessee state prison system.

He put the car in gear and made a U-turn. We drove for a few minutes and my vision gradually started to clear. The trooper had his hat off now and I could see his eyes and part of his face in the rearview. There was something familiar about this guy. I thought maybe I'd seen him before, but I couldn't remember when or where. Then it came to me. It was Garland. His last name escaped me, but it was Garland from the poker game at Ted Grayson's house.

The guy with the gun in his boot.

"Garland. It's me, Nicholas Colt."

"Who?"

"Nicholas Colt. From the card game at Ted Grayson's house."

He turned around and took a quick glance at me. "Nicholas Colt. I didn't recognize you. You look like death warmed over. What happened?"

"That's what I've been trying to tell you. I was kidnapped."

"No shit?"

"No shit. Ever heard of a white supremacist sect called the Harvest Angels?"

"Can't say that I have."

"They have a compound right here on this mountain. It's just a house, really, and a few single-wides, but they seem to be pretty organized."

I told him about my adopted daughter being abducted three years ago and her sister being murdered, and I told him about the Lamb murders and the tilted crosses, about coming to Tennessee to investigate the disappearance of Derek Wahl, about Derek showing up at my house in Florida and me killing him in self-defense. I told him about putting Juliet and Brittney on a plane to the Philippines. I told him about Lester and Earl and the big guy they called Bear, about being abducted and escaping and finding Pete Strong dangling from a tree branch.

"Do you know the name of the leader?" he said.

"I don't. He says he's an old friend of mine, but I swear I've never seen him before. I just call him Stoneface. He doesn't smile a lot."

Garland laughed. "Stoneface. That's a good one."

He slowed and made a left turn onto a winding gravel road that led back up the hill. He switched on his brights, bathing a wide swatch of the dead winter landscape in harsh white light.

In a few minutes, we stopped at a steel gate.

On either side of it were three strands of barbed wire.

CHAPTER TWENTY-FIVE

I fell to my side and started kicking at the door, but all I managed to do was strain my left hamstring. Garland was taking me back to Stoneface's compound. The motherfucker was taking me back.

"You're an officer of the law," I said. "How can you be part of this insanity?"

"Shut up."

He got out and used a key to open the padlock on the gate, drove through, and got out again and locked it.

The lights were on at Stoneface's house. Garland cruised around to the rear of the building, put the car in park, and killed the engine. He drew his pistol and opened the back door and told me to get out.

"I'm not going in there. Go ahead and shoot me. I'm not going back."

"Get the fuck out. Now."

I didn't move. He pulled out a walkie-talkie and said something into it and a few minutes later a pair of goons similar to the ones I'd killed in the woods came and dragged me kicking and screaming into the house. They stripped my clothes off, scrubbed my body with soap and water, put a hospital gown on me, and strapped me back into the chair in the lab. A guy in a white coat came in and started an IV in my left arm and hung a saline drip. He connected some tubing to a bottle of the stuff that looked like chocolate milk and resumed my feeding. He inserted another urinary catheter, turned the lights off, and left me in the dark. I was exhausted. I closed my eyes and tried to sleep but my leg wouldn't let me. It was throbbing like a disco. An hour passed, maybe two, and the door opened and the lights came on. Stoneface walked in and sat at the table across from me.

"What's your name?" he said.

"I need something for pain," I said. My mouth was dry, my voice raspy.

"What's your name?"

"You know my name. Why are you playing fucking games with me?"

"What's your name?"

"Nicholas Colt. You want my rank and serial number?"

"Several men are dead because of you," he said.

He stared at me for a minute and then walked to the medicine cart and drew something into a syringe and injected it into one of the ports on my IV line. My left hamstring stopped hurting immediately.

But the medication did more than ease my pain. I felt happier than I'd ever felt in my life. I felt as though I'd just made the winning touchdown at the Super Bowl. The world seemed wondrous and magical and full of possibilities.

"What was that?" I said.

"Do you like it?"

"It worked."

"Where are Brittney and Juliet?"

"Fuck you."

He turned the lights off and left the room. I was alone in the dark again. I tried to concentrate on my predicament and figure a way out of it, but my brain wasn't working right. Not right at all.

I kept thinking about the Beatles' song, "Lucy in the Sky with Diamonds." Tangerine trees and marmalade skies. Marshmallow pies. Kaleidoscope eyes. Big Mac and fries. I was hungry. I was fucking starving, and the formula being pumped into my gut wasn't cutting it.

"Hey, I need something to eat," I shouted.

The door opened and the lights came on and the guy with the white coat who'd connected all my tubes earlier came in.

"What would you like?" he said.

"A Big Mac and fries. Wait. Better make it two."

"Two Big Macs?"

"Yes."

"And fries?"

"Yes."

He switched the lights off on his way out.

A motorized movie screen came down from the ceiling and an episode of *Flash Gordon* came on. The old black-and-white television show. It was an episode titled "Deadline at Noon." The villain used a time machine to travel back twelve hundred years to the 1950s and plant a bomb that would blow the Earth up twelve hundred years in the future. Flash and crew had an hour to travel back and find the bomb and deactivate it and save the world.

They found the bomb buried in a pile of rubble in Berlin. It was about the size of a birthday cake and it was going to make the planet pop like a firecracker. Flash started working on defusing the device. Somehow he knew exactly how to do this. He had less than a minute before the world went blammo. The suspense was killing me.

The screen went black and the lights came on and the guy with the white coat came back in carrying a white bag with golden arches on it and a large drink cup. He rolled an adjustable table to my side, unwrapped one of the Big Macs and spread the wrapper out and put the sandwich on the wrapper and dumped the order of fries next to it.

"I didn't know what you wanted to drink," he said. "Is Coke all right?"

"Coke's fine. What's with the old episode of *Flash Gordon*?"

He ignored my question. "You want ketchup?"

"Yes."

He opened a package of ketchup and squeezed it onto the wrapper next to the fries.

"Which hand do you eat with?"

"My right."

He unbuckled my right hand.

"Enjoy," he said.

I lifted the all-beef patties special sauce lettuce cheese pickles onions on a sesame seed bun and took a big bite. I picked up three fries and dragged them through the ketchup and stuffed them into my mouth. I licked the salt off my fingers. I went at the meal with intensity, finishing the Big Mac and most of the fries in under five minutes. The man in the white coat unwrapped the second burger and I wolfed that one down and ate the rest of the fries and drank the Coke. He gathered my trash and stuffed it all into the big white bag with golden arches on it. He rolled the table away and secured my arm back and turned the lights off and left the room. I fell asleep and dreamed about whizzing through the galaxy with a rocket strapped to my ass.

CHAPTER TWENTY-SIX

Rule #8 in Nicholas Colt's *Philosophy of Life*: You can't always get what you want. But, if you try sometimes you just might get what you need.

I stole rule #8 from a poet named Mick Jagger.

I woke up in severe pain. The back of my left thigh felt like a hot chunk of iron pulled from the fire and slammed onto the anvil for hammering. I must have actually pulled the muscle, or maybe even ruptured it. Along with that were the normal aches and pains any forty-eight-year-old man has when he Fosbury Flops over a barbed wire fence and strips his dead friend naked and spends hours traipsing through the wilderness searching for a way out of a nightmare. I had cuts and bruises and blisters and abrasions and a headache and a sore throat. My entire body was one big boo-boo.

I needed another one of those shots.

I sat there and thought about it. The more I thought about it, the more I wanted it.

Stoneface came in with a female assistant and a surgery cart.

"What's your name?" Stoneface said.

"It hasn't changed."

"What's your name?"

"Nicholas Colt."

"Since you're eating, I'm going to remove your feeding tube. If you start cooperating in other ways, I'll remove the urinary catheter as well."

"I need something for pain," I said.

"I thought you might."

He reached into his lab coat pocket and pulled out a syringe already loaded with medication. He injected it into my IV, and within seconds, I was blanketed with a euphoria that was nearly orgasmic. The pain in my leg was gone, and I didn't have a care in the world.

"Better?" Stoneface said.

"Yes. Thank you."

It only took him a few minutes to remove the feeding tube. The procedure didn't hurt. I sat there and watched as though it were happening to somebody else.

"There," Stoneface said. "All done." He taped some gauze over the wound.

"I'm hungry," I said. "Can I have some breakfast?"

"Certainly. What would you like this morning?"

"Ham. Ham and eggs and toast. And coffee."

He turned to his assistant and asked if she could arrange that and she said no problem and left the room.

"Why are you being so nice to me all of a sudden?" I said.

"Was I not nice to you before?"

"You wanted me to eat that green paste. When I refused—"

"Let's just say my plans for you have changed," he said.

He snapped off his surgical gloves and tossed them into the metal trash can by the door on his way out.

The ham and eggs came and I ate them and drank the coffee and someone took the tray away when I was finished. This time, both my arms were unbuckled and the attendant didn't strap them back when he left the room. Stoneface probably had a hidden camera somewhere and was watching to see if I would try to escape.

I didn't.

I wanted to get out of there more than anything in the world, but there was no way I could run on the bum leg. I wasn't sure I could even walk. I decided to play Stoneface's little game for a while and see what happened. He'd said he had new plans for me. Maybe, if I played along, I could earn enough trust to be completely loosened from my bonds. Then I could shove those new plans up his ass.

The lights went dim and the movie screen came down and *Flash Gordon* came on again. It was the same episode, about the bomb that was going to blow the world up. I studied the images, looking away from the action, scanning the edges of the background scenery, trying to find any evidence that the film had been tampered with. Maybe Stoneface was trying to brainwash me with subliminal messages embedded in the video. Why else would he show me the same episode twice? Then again, maybe it was just another form of torture. Maybe he was going to slowly bore me to death with cheesy 1950s television.

I saw the ending this time and, just as I suspected, Flash saved the world with only seconds to spare. Flash and his teammates, a pair of scientists named Dale Arden and Hans Zarkov, had a good laugh about the close shave. They didn't break a sweat or piss their pants or anything. They were cool as cucumbers.

Dale Arden was a beautiful woman. She reminded me of a young Donna Wahl. I wondered if Donna was busy putting together a civil suit against me for killing her brother. I didn't see any way she could win, but a lawsuit would cost me some money and make my life miserable for a while and maybe that would be enough for her.

Revenge. Some great thinker once said that anyone who seeks it keeps their own wounds festering. Something like that. It makes sense, but like all sayings, it's easy to say and harder to live. Revenge was part of the reason I came to Tennessee in the first place. I wasn't proud of it, hated to admit it, but it was the truth. My first wife Susan and our baby daughter Harmony come to me in dreams sometimes. Especially Susan. I think it's her laughter I miss the most. I can hear it in my dreams.

A guy came in and wrapped my sore leg with an ACE bandage. He didn't say anything. He just came in and did it and left. A few minutes later, Stoneface came in with another syringe in his hand.

"What's your name?"

"I don't want that," I said, gesturing toward the syringe.

"What's your name?"

"Nicholas Colt."

"This is your pain medicine."

"My leg's not hurting that bad right now," I said. "I don't need it."

"Better to keep the pain at bay. It's easier to control if you don't let it get too severe."

He moved to inject the contents of the syringe into my IV line. I pulled my arm away.

"I said I don't want it."

His expression didn't change. It never changed.

"I want you to have the medication," he said. "And as you know, there's no point in resisting. I'll get what I want one way or another."

I thought about yanking the IV out of by arm, but if I did one of Stoneface's goons would just come in and start another one. He was right. There was no point in resisting. I relaxed and allowed him to give me the injection.

The euphoria washed over me like a sweet warm wave. I was in heaven. I didn't care that I was being held captive in a compound populated by lunatics. I didn't care that the leader, the emotionless man with the face of stone, stood there staring at me now with those icy blue eyes of his. Everything was cool. Everything was all right.

I looked at Stoneface and smiled. "You were right," I said. "I feel much better now."

"Good," he said. He reached down and unbuckled the straps on my legs. "Try to stand."

I stood. I felt a twinge of pain, but it wasn't bad.

"Feels good to be out of that chair," I said. "Mind if I walk around a little bit?"

"Go ahead."

I walked the perimeter of the room. It was a fairly large space, eighteen by thirty, I guessed. There was a sink and a long countertop against one wall and some metal cabinets with locks on the handles. The medication cart had locks on it as well, although I didn't remember Stoneface ever using a key to access it. Maybe he left it unlocked for convenience. There was a computer, and a bookcase filled with old-looking medical reference books. If there was a hidden camera somewhere, it must have been hidden well. I did four laps, limping pretty badly on the last one.

I eased back down in the chair.

"How does it feel?" Stoneface said.

"Better."

"Good. I'm going to let you start exercising some every day. Supervised, of course."

"You don't trust me?"

"About as far as I can throw you. But we're going to work on that. Like I said, I have plans for you. I see great things in your future."

"Mind filling me in on these great plans?"

"Not yet."

"Why not?"

"I wouldn't want to spoil the surprise."

He left the room and the screen came down and I rode the narcotic buzz while Flash and Dale and Dr. Zarkov saved the world again.

CHAPTER TWENTY-SEVEN

Weeks went by. There was no clock in the room, so I never knew if it was day or night, but I had constructed a calendar in my mind and I tried to keep track of the passing days. My calendar said April 1. I had no way of knowing if that was right or not, but I figured it was close.

I had been in the compound for over a month. The hole in my belly had closed up and my urinary catheter was gone and my left hamstring had completely healed. No more fluids, but I still had an intravenous access on the inside of my left upper arm called a PICC line. It allowed me to get medications and have blood samples drawn. I was getting three hot meals a day, whatever I wanted, and I had earned the privilege to walk to the bathroom by myself.

At some point, the man I had been referring to as Stoneface told me his name was Brother John. He had brought an exercise bike and some dumbbells into the room. I didn't have much else to occupy my time, so I rode the bike and lifted the weights and did push-ups and sit-ups to complete exhaustion. I did it all day every day, like training for an event. I had the bike programmed to a plateau program and was ten minutes into the thirty-minute workout when Brother John came in holding a small pouch. I stopped pedaling and dismounted the machine.

"What's your name?" Brother John said.

I had to think about it. "Alexander Maddox," I said. "But my friends call me Maddog. Or just Dog."

"Sorry to interrupt your session, Maddog."

"It's all right. I'll just start over in a few minutes."

"I wanted to give you this."

He handed me the pouch. I opened it and pulled out a very nice gold wristwatch, a Rolex.

"This is a nice watch," I said.

"I want you to have it."

I put it on my left wrist and snapped the clasp shut. It was a little loose. I looked at the face and for the first time in a long time saw the time and date. It was Tuesday, April 12, 7:47 a.m.

"Is this date right?" I said.

"Yes."

Somehow, I had lost nearly two weeks.

"Thank you," I said. "It'll be nice to be able to keep track of the time."

"You're welcome. It's your reward for doing so well these past few weeks."

The watch was nice, but I was only truly interested in one reward. "Can I have my shot now?" I said.

"I've decided we need to cut back on that," he said.

"I need it. The last time you decided to cut back, I had a seizure and almost died."

My fingers started trembling at the thought of doing without.

"Well, maybe we can work something out," Brother John said. "I want you to do something for me."

"What?"

He motioned for me to follow him. We exited the room and made a couple of turns and he opened a door and led me down a long hallway that reminded me of a hotel corridor. We came to a room with a 3 on the door and he opened it with a key and we walked in. It was a small room. There was a table and two chairs. On the table there was a black box the size of a dictionary with a toggle switch and a dial on it. A bundle of wires connected to the back of the box snaked across the table and disappeared into the wall.

"What's this?" I said.

"On the other side of the wall, there's a man hooked up to the machine. When you flip the toggle switch, with the dial on zero, he will receive a very mild electrical shock. As you turn the dial clockwise to one, two, three, et cetera, the shock intensifies. Anything above six is potentially lethal."

"Forget it. I'm not doing it."

"Then you're not getting your shot."

I took a deep breath. "What did this guy do to deserve to be tortured?"

"That's irrelevant."

Brother John sat in one of the chairs. He motioned for me to take the other one. I sat down and laced my fingers together to keep them from shaking.

"Why are you doing this to me?"

"Go ahead. Flip the switch."

I didn't want to hurt anyone, but I needed the shot. With the dial on zero, the shock would be mild and if I just went ahead and did it, I could get it over with and get my medicine and resume my workout and have a nice breakfast.

I flipped the switch.

A loud moan emanated from the other side of the wall, something you might hear in the waiting room of a dentist's office. I flipped the switch to the OFF position and the moaning stopped. I felt nauseated and my left pinky was jittering like a rattlesnake tail.

"Now turn the dial to one and flip the switch again," Brother John said.

Maybe one wouldn't hurt that bad. It would only be for a few seconds. I wouldn't let it go on any longer than that. I turned the dial and flipped the switch and the guy on the other side of the wall screamed and shouted as if someone had thrown him off a roof.

I turned off the switch. I picked up the wastebasket beside my chair and started dry-heaving into it.

"I need my goddamn shot," I said.

Brother John got up and came around and emptied a syringe into my PICC line. I felt better immediately. We walked back to my room and he left me there in my chair.

I didn't feel like exercising anymore.

CHAPTER TWENTY-EIGHT

Thursday, April 28. Breakfast came and I ate and drank some coffee. After breakfast *Flash Gordon* came on and after that I exercised and took a shower and walked to room 3 and tortured the guy on the other side of the wall. That had become my routine. Eat, watch *Flash Gordon*, exercise, take a shower, walk to room 3. Eat, watch *Flash Gordon*, exercise, take a shower, walk to room 3. Eat, watch *Flash Gordon*, exercise, take a shower, walk to room 3. My name was Alexander Maddox, and that was my life.

Brother John came in around eleven. It had been twelve hours since I'd had a shot, and I needed one badly.

"What's your name?"

"Where's my shot?"

"What's your name?"

"Alexander Maddox. My friends call me Maddog. Where's my shot?"

"How far have you been turning the dial?"

"Four," I said. "Same as always."

"I want you to go up to seven today."

"It'll kill him," I said.

"I want you to go up to seven today."

"I'm not a murderer."

"What's your name?"

"I can't do it."

"What's your name?"

"Alexander Maddox. My friends call me Maddog."

"Am I your friend?"

"Yes."

"I want you to go up to seven today."

I needed the shot. I couldn't function without it. I got up and walked to room 3. Brother John followed me. We sat at the table.

"Give him one at zero," Brother John said.

I flipped the toggle. The guy on the other side of the wall moaned in agony.

"This isn't right," I said.

"Turn the dial to seven."

"What's his name?" I said.

"His name?"

"If I'm going to kill someone for you, at least tell me who it is."

"He's an enemy. His name's not important."

"If I turn the dial to seven and flip the switch, you'll give me my shot?"

"I have it right here in my pocket."

I turned the dial to seven and flipped the switch. The guy on the other side of the wall made a long and continuous guttural grunt. It sounded like he was straining to take a shit. I wanted it to stop. I wanted to switch off the voltage, but I couldn't. If I switched off the voltage, I wouldn't get my shot, and not getting my shot wasn't an option. I had to have it. I sat there and listened to the poor motherfucker for about thirty seconds, and then it was over.

"Is he dead?" I said.

"What do you think?"

"I want my shot now."

"Where's Dale?"

"Who?"

"Your girl. She's in the Philippines. She's in trouble. I need an address."

"Dale. From the show?"

"Yes. She's your girl. Don't you remember?"

My hands were trembling. "I don't remember any address," I said.

"When you remember, then you'll get your shot."

I rose and grabbed him by the lapels of his lab coat. "You lying son of a bitch!"

A couple of muscle heads came in and pulled me off him and dragged me to my room. They strapped me into the chair and left the room and a few minutes later, *Flash Gordon* came on.

I had a feeling I had lost some of my privileges.

CHAPTER TWENTY-NINE

I fell asleep for a while and had a weird dream. I was fourteen years old and my name was Maddog. I left my house and went out into the night and turned into a wolf. I went trotting down a dirt road naked and hairy in the moonlight. Something smelled delicious, something not far away, something just around the bend.

The heavy foliage lining the road opened to a clearing, a fenced pasture where a dozen or so goats grazed. Beyond the meadow was a barn, and beyond that a two-story farmhouse, white with black shutters.

It was like a living buffet spread out before me, an abundance of food there for the taking. I only needed to choose which little goat to murder.

A white one stood off by itself, apart from the group. That was the one.

I quietly climbed over the wooden fence and slinked through the dewy grass.

My breakfast was only a few feet away from me now. Its big black eyes looked out docilely at nothing, and its mouth curled up in a cute little smile as it chewed its cud. The end was coming soon, but it just stood there, oblivious, unaware of my presence. I began to salivate. My heart pounded with anticipation.

I pounced.

My teeth sank deeply into its throat before it could make a sound. In my peripheral vision, I saw the rest of the herd stampeding toward the barn. I wondered if they mourned the loss. I didn't care. I had a single objective, to fill my belly as quickly as possible with the life struggling beneath me.

I clamped down tighter, and the goat went limp. It wasn't dead yet, but it lay there relaxed, resigned to its fate now.

Instinctually, I knew the animal's heart needed to stop before I began feasting. Otherwise, too much blood would be pumped out and lost in the ground. With a jerk of my head, I snapped the trachea and after a few labored wheezes, the goat died. I didn't waste any time after that. I bit into the tender skin on the lower belly and ripped a midline gash. The coppery scent of fresh whole blood rose steamily into the predawn mist, and the beautiful coils of intestines glistened in the moonlight.

I lapped the blood pooling at the center of my crude incision before it had a chance to coagulate. I greedily chomped into the entrails, and then gobbled one tangy kidney and part of the liver. I peeled the hairy skin away from one of the hind legs and went to work on a length of muscle and fat. I tore the flesh away in strips, slurped it into my mouth like strings of spaghetti. The meat was warm and juicy and fresh. It was the best thing I had ever tasted.

I heard footsteps. I looked toward the house, saw that someone was on the wooden porch. It was a man wearing overalls and a straw hat. Our eyes locked and he started toward me and I scampered away into the woods.

I woke up sweating. Brother John was standing in front of me with a syringe in his hand. The straps on my arms and legs had been unbuckled.

"What's your name?"

"Alexander Maddox. My friends call me Maddog. Or just Dog."

"Tell me the address," he said.

"I don't remember. I swear I don't." I was shaking all over. It felt like a million cockroaches were under my skin running relays.

"Tell me the address, and I'll give you the shot."

"If I knew the address, I would tell you," I said. "Believe me, I would tell you."

He stood there silently staring into space for a few seconds, and then said, "For some reason, I believe you. I think we're ready to proceed with phase six."

Phase six. I didn't know what the fuck he was talking about. I just wanted my shot. He could have proceeded with phase fifty million and it would have been fine with me. He left the room and came back carrying an electric guitar and a small amplifier. He plugged the amp into the wall and plugged the guitar into the amp. He handed me the guitar. It was a Fender Stratocaster.

"What do you want me to do with this?" I said.

"I want you to play it, of course."

"Do I know how to play the guitar?"

"Yes. Your name is Maddog Maddox, and you're an excellent guitar player."

He handed me a pick. To my amazement, my trembling fingers knew exactly where to go. I started strumming chords, and I even knew their names. *E...A...B...*

I strummed a twelve-bar blues progression effortlessly, and then started playing lead notes. Before long, I was bending and tapping strings and making the instrument cry with the tremolo bar.

"I can really play," I said.

"Yes. You're even better than I remember."

"Than you remember?"

"I'm going to leave you a CD, and I want you to learn all the songs on it. There are twenty. Once you learn them all, I have a job for you."

"What job?"

"We'll discuss it after you learn the songs."

"Can I have my shot now?"

"Ah. Of course."

He uncapped the port on my PICC line and administered the medication.

CHAPTER THIRTY

There was a set of headphones by the computer. I carried the CD and the guitar and amp over there and loaded the CD and listened to it through the headphones. It was a compilation of rock and pop songs from the sixties and seventies. Songs like "Hang on Sloopy" and "Margaritaville" and "Proud Mary." I listened to all twenty of them and then started playing along with the guitar. Somehow, I instinctively knew the chords and the changes and the lead riffs. It came to me as easily as breathing.

I went through the songs a few more times until I had them down pat. One of the guys came in and asked if I was hungry and I looked at my watch and saw it was time for supper. I'd missed lunch completely. I asked if he would bring me a salad and some fried chicken and he said he would. As he was leaving I added iced tea with lemon to the order and he said OK.

I started working my way through the songs again. I finished "Smoke on the Water" and was waiting for the intro to "Jumping Jack Flash" when I turned and noticed Brother John standing behind me with his arms crossed. I took the headphones off.

"How's it going?" he said.

"Great. It's like I've been playing these songs all my life."

"Splendid. I'm very proud of you."

He patted me on the back. It made me feel good that he was proud of me.

"Let me see your fingers," he said.

I showed him the fingertips of my left hand. They were red and swollen and blistered.

"They don't hurt that bad," I said.

"I want you to stop for the day. In fact, I want you stop for a couple of days and give your fingers a chance to heal."

"You're the boss," I said. I looked at my watch. I reminded him it was time for another shot, and he went and drew it up, gave it to me, and then left the room.

My fried chicken and salad and iced tea with lemon came. I put everything on the rolling table and rolled the table to my chair and ate supper by myself. I had eaten every meal by myself for as long as I could remember. It was a lonely way to live. It would have been nice to have someone to talk to, but I couldn't remember it ever being any other way so I wondered how I could miss something I never had. Brother John had said that Dale from the show was my girl. She was a beautiful woman. If she was my girl, I should be with her, I thought. Someday I would be with her, maybe after this job Brother John had for me, whatever it was. I longed for some companionship. I wished I could remember the address in the Philippines. If she was there, I wanted to be there with her. I tried to think while I ate, but for the life of me I couldn't remember anything. All I knew was that my name was Alexander Maddox and my friends called me Maddog and I was an excellent guitar player.

It was hard to eat with one hand, but the blisters on my left fingertips screamed bloody hell every time they came in contact with the hot greasy chicken. I managed to finish, and the same guy who had brought the food in came and took the trash away. He didn't say anything. The guys never said much. They were all business.

The lights went down and the show came on and I sat back and relaxed and watched it. I paid special attention to Dale this time. Brother John had said that she was my girl. She was certainly a beautiful woman.

After the show, I exercised for a while and then took a shower and shaved. It was almost time for my weekly haircut. I had a crew cut, like all the other guys, and Brother John insisted on a clean-shaven face. There was a tattoo of an angel on my left arm. I had no recollection of how it got there. Maybe I had been to Margaritaville at the time, like Jimmy Buffet. It was a nice tattoo. The angel's wings were spread, and every feather had been drawn with painstaking detail. There was a circle on the angel's chest and the number 88 inside the circle. The angel had a crew cut and a clean-shaven face.

Saturday the barber came and gave me a haircut. A few minutes after he left, Brother John came and gave me my shot and looked at my fingers.

"How do they feel?" he said.

"Great. I'm ready to play some more."

"Good. I'm going to take you on a little trip in a few days."

"Is this the job you were telling me about?"

"Yes."

"So what is it you want me to do?"

"I want you to do what I tell you to do. Nothing more, nothing less."

He turned and walked out of the room.

CHAPTER THIRTY-ONE

I spent the next few days learning more songs, this time from a Christian rock group called Testimony. Brother John had sent them a promo package with my picture and a sample of my playing, and they had invited me to come to LA and work with them on their new album.

I was in my room composing the lead guitar solo for a song called "Need to Know" when one of the guys wheeled in two Marshall speaker cabinets and a Marshall amplifier head and a multi-effects pedal. He positioned the gear near the computer and cabled everything together. Shortly after he left, Brother John came in and gave me my shot.

"What's your name?"

"Alexander Maddox, but my friends call me Maddog. Or just Dog."

"How's it going?"

"I'm working on the lead part to the last song," I said. "I'll be ready by the end of the day."

"Excellent. How do you like your new equipment?"

"It's big."

"It's called a Marshall full stack. The effects unit is a Boss GT-Ten. World-class gear for a world-class player."

"Thank you. It's very nice."

"I want you to practice with it, fiddle around with the effects, and so forth. We're going to pack up and leave for California day after tomorrow."

"We're flying out there?"

"No, we'll be going in a van. A couple of my men will be driving us."

"Is it a long drive?"

"It is, but I assure you the van is very comfortable. Think of it as an adventure."

"OK."

He left and I resumed my practice session, using the new amplifier and the effects pedal. Everything sounded superb, much better than the small practice amp I'd been using.

I kept trying to remember how I became such a good musician. Occasionally, a little snippet would come to me in a flash, like a quick edit on a movie screen. In one of these jittery images, I saw myself as a very young man, twenty-four or twenty-five, with hair to my shoulders and a full beard. I wore bell-bottom jeans and a denim jacket with the sleeves cut off. I was holding a red hollow-body electric guitar, and there was a white bandana tied around my head. I saw it clear as day and I knew it was me, but then it dissolved and disappeared as quickly as it had come.

Apparently, I had been playing the guitar for a long time. I wanted to know about my past. I decided I wasn't going to practice anymore or go to Los Angeles or cooperate in any way until Brother John told me some things. I sat in my chair and waited. One of the guys came and asked what I wanted for supper. I told him I wanted to speak with Brother John and he said OK.

Brother John came in a few minutes later.

"What's your name?" he said.

"Alexander Maddox, but my friends call me Maddog."

"Why did you stop playing?"

"I want to know who I am."

"You just told me who you are. Your name is Alexander—"

"I want to know about my history. Where was I born? Who are my parents? Why am I here? Why do I have a tattoo of an angel on my arm? How did I learn how to play the guitar? I can't remember any of that stuff."

"I'll tell you everything you want to know," he said. "After our trip to California. There's going to be a big event on Friday, and we'll be heading back home early that morning. I'll tell you everything then. It's going to be glorious, Maddog. You'll see."

"I want to know now."

"Not possible."

"Why not?"

"Haven't I been good to you? Haven't I given you everything you want?"

"That's beside the point," I said. "Everyone has a right to know where they came from. I want to know, and I want to know now."

He got up and left the room without saying another word. The lights dimmed and the screen came down and the show came on. *Flash Gordon.* "Deadline at Noon." I had seen it a thousand times. I picked up the Fender Stratocaster by the neck and started swinging it like an ax at the projection screen. Before I was able to destroy the guitar and the screen, two guys came in and strapped me into my chair. Brother John came in and gave me a shot, but it wasn't my usual shot. Everything went black and when I woke up, we were in the van heading for LA.

CHAPTER THIRTY-TWO

Brother John and I sat in a pair of fancy reclining seats bolted to the floor behind the driver and the guy riding shotgun. The headliner had been fitted with faux wood paneling and recessed LED lights and drop-down DVD monitors. There weren't any side windows. A steel lattice partition divided the passenger section from the cargo section, and through it I could see some suitcases and the Marshall speaker cabinets.

I looked at my watch. It was Monday, May 9, 10:50 a.m. It had been over thirty-six hours since I'd had a shot. The insects were dancing under my skin again.

"Where are we?" I said.

Brother John looked up from the book he was reading. "What's your name?"

"Alexander Maddox. My friends call me Maddog. Where are we?"

"We're in Oklahoma," he said. "We got an early start. We'll stop for lunch in Oklahoma City."

"I need my shot. And I need to take a piss."

Brother John reached under his seat and grabbed a leather satchel. It looked like the bag that Doc carried on the TV show *Gunsmoke*. He unwrapped a fresh syringe, drew the medication from a vial, wiped the port on my PICC line with an alcohol swab, and screwed the syringe onto the port. He pushed the plunger slowly and the subdermal cockroaches that had become the bane of my existence stopped doing the Watusi and once again everything was right with the world. Everything except my bladder. He instructed the driver to take the next exit and he did and we all got out and took a bathroom break at the Shell station. The guy who had been driving filled the gas tank. There was a Shoney's across the street and Brother John said we might as well eat lunch now instead of having to stop again.

The drivers sat at one booth and Brother John and I at another. Brother John suggested we all choose the buffet. Everything looked fresh and there were a lot of choices. I had a salad and some meatloaf and mashed potatoes. The waitress brought me an iced tea and Brother John a Coca-Cola.

"Will there be anything else?" she asked.

"That should do it," Brother John said.

She set the check on the table. "Just pay up front whenever you're ready."

She smiled and walked away.

"How's the meatloaf?" Brother John said.

"A little greasy, but good."

"We should be settled in LA by this time tomorrow."

"You never did tell me why we're going there," I said.

"You're going to record some songs with the group Testimony. I thought I made that clear."

"Sure, but you also said there's going to be some big event Friday. Today's Monday. That doesn't give us much time to record an album."

"Very astute of you, Maddog. You're right. We won't be sticking around for the whole album."

I took a bite of meatloaf and washed it down with some tea. "So what's the big event?"

"Like I said, it's going to be glorious. That's all you need to know for now."

We finished our meal and the drivers grabbed a mint and a toothpick and walked outside while Brother John and I waited for someone to come to the register. A guy with a bad haircut and a nametag that said Barry Collins, Assistant Manager, finally came and rang us up.

"Was everything all right?" he said.

"Fine," Brother John said.

I thought about saying something about the meatloaf being a little greasy, but I didn't.

We walked out to the van. The drivers had switched places. The one who had been driving before was now in the front passenger's seat. We had a full tank of gas and I knew it would be a long time before we stopped again, so I did a few stretches before climbing into my seat.

CHAPTER THIRTY-THREE

As promised, we were in LA by lunchtime on Tuesday. From the interstate, we took the San Bernardino Freeway and got off on Hollywood Boulevard. Brother John told the driver to take a right on Vine, and a few minutes later we parked at a meter in front of a tall circular building with a sign on top that said Capitol Records.

"Come with me, Maddog," Brother John said.

There were stars on the sidewalk, but I didn't recognize any of the names. We walked through the front door and into the lobby of the building. At the reception desk, there was an attractive young lady with long blonde hair wearing a navy-blue business suit and a telephone headset. Her nametag said Ericka.

"May I help you?"

"I need to speak with Bob Watson," Brother John said.

Ericka thumbed through some papers on a clipboard. "Bob's in a session right now. I could leave him a message if you—"

"I know he's in a session. That's why we're here. Just tell him Brother John is waiting in the lobby."

She punched some numbers into her phone base, but nobody answered.

"I'll send him a text," she said.

She sent Bob Watson a text, and his message back said he would be down in a few minutes. Brother John and I sat in a pair of leather armchairs and waited.

"Who's Bob Watson?" I said.

"The producer. Talented guy. Look at any *Billboard* from the last twenty years and you're going to see his name somewhere between the covers."

The lobby was decorated with potted plants and gold records and photographs of famous musicians: Sinatra sporting a fedora, standing behind a microphone with his hands in his pockets; Dean Martin in a black tuxedo, holding a cigarette and a glass of whiskey; the Beach Boys, young and clean-cut, wearing matching striped shirts. I was admiring a shot of John, Paul, George, and Ringo when the elevator dinged and out stepped a man wearing white pants and a blue polo and tinted glasses. Midfifties, tall and slim, tanned and toned. His sandy blond hairpiece was barely detectable.

Brother John stood and shook the man's hand. "Great to see you, Bob."

"You too, my friend. Is this your guitar player?"

"Yes. Bob Watson, meet Alexander 'Maddog' Maddox."

I stood and shook Bob Watson's hand. "Pleased to meet you," I said.

Bob smiled, revealing a mouthful of porcelain veneers. "Same here. I've heard nothing but good things about you. We're just laying some drum tracks right now, but I'd like to get started on some rhythm guitar this evening. How's that sound?"

"Sounds great," I said.

"We'll go grab some lunch and get settled in at the hotel," Brother John said. "Can we go ahead and unload Maddog's amp and stuff while we're here?"

"Absolutely," Bob said. "We're on the eighth floor, Studio B. Need someone to wheel it up for you?"

"I have a couple of roadies with me, but thanks."

"Bitchin'. See you guys around six."

"We'll be here."

We said good-bye and headed back outside. As we strolled past the reception desk, Ericka smiled and winked at me. I couldn't help but grin.

—∞—

We checked in at the Beverly Hills Hotel. It was a fancy place, everything plush and expensive. My room had a king-size bed and a desk and a leather couch. There was a flat-screen television and a Jacuzzi and a large balcony with chairs and a table and a big umbrella.

"This is nice," I said.

"I'll be next door," Brother John said. "The rooms open to a suite if you want to visit."

"OK."

I didn't want to visit. I couldn't remember the last time I'd had any privacy, and I wanted to relish every minute of it.

"You ready to go get some lunch?" he said.

"I was thinking about just calling room service and hanging out here."

"Suit yourself. I'll see you later this afternoon, then."

"I need my shot," I said.

He left for a few minutes, and came back with the syringe and pushed the medicine into my PICC.

"We'll leave about five thirty to go back to the studio," he said.

"OK."

I called room service and ordered a turkey bacon club and French fries and a bottle of Perrier. I watched *Bonanza* on TV while I ate. Amazing the trouble those guys could get in and out of in the span of an hour. After lunch I climbed into the bathtub and ran the jets for a while and then just soaked and relaxed. The bars of soap were larger than you get at most places. They were embossed with *The Beverly Hills Hotel* logo and smelled like cinnamon. The wrapper said they were made from goat's milk and olive oil. It was damn good soap. It made my skin feel silky smooth.

I watched some more television after my bath and fell asleep on the couch. I woke up to an infomercial about a revolutionary new herbal supplement that would transform you from a fat and stupid lazy sloth into a rich, sexy supermodel practically overnight. All that for only three easy payments of $39.99. Lifelong happiness for a hundred and twenty bucks. It seemed like a bargain to me.

I picked my Rolex up off the coffee table. Five fifteen. Almost time to go. As I went to put the watch on my wrist, something caught my eye. There was an inscription engraved on the back plate. It was barely visible. I had to squint to make it out.

It said *To Pete. All my love, Denise.*

CHAPTER THIRTY-FOUR

At five thirty someone knocked on my door. I answered. It was
Brother John.

"Why aren't you ready?" he said.

I was still wearing the *BHH* terry cloth bathrobe I'd found in
the closet.

"Who's Pete?" I said.

"Who?"

"And Denise. Who are they?"

The names sounded familiar, but I couldn't for the life of me
visualize the people they belonged to. It was frustrating, like having a word on the tip of your tongue and not being able to come
up with it.

"I don't know what you're talking about," Brother John said.

I handed him the watch. "Look at the back plate. Look really
close."

He looked really close. "To Pete. All my love, Denise. Is that
what you're talking about?"

"Yeah. Who are they?"

"Well, I'm afraid I'm busted," he said. "You see, the watch wasn't new. I bought it at a pawnshop."

"But those names sound really familiar to me. Like…déjà vu or something."

"I don't know what to tell you. Anyway, we need to get going."

"I'll be ready in five minutes," I said.

"Meet me in the lobby."

I opened a suitcase and chose a pair of black jeans and a white Tommy Bahama button-down. I put those on and a pair of loafers and walked to the lobby. I left the hard case behind and carried the Strat in a black vinyl gig bag.

I followed Brother John to a Mercedes convertible in the parking lot.

"Where'd this come from?" I said.

"You didn't think we were going to ride around in that van the whole time, did you? This is a rental. Pretty nice, don't you think?"

"Bitchin'," I said.

We took Sunset to Vine and turned into a twenty-four-hour lot across the street from the Capitol tower. Brother John handed the attendant a voucher. The barrier arm rose and we drove through and found a spot. We walked across the street, went inside, and took the elevator to the eighth floor. When we stepped out there was an overhead sign that said QUIET—RECORDING AREA—OBSERVE RECORDING LIGHTS.

We were quiet.

We walked down a hallway with more gold records on the walls and more pictures of bands and solo artists. The RECORDING light over the doorway to studio B wasn't on, so we walked on in. Bob Watson was sitting on a sofa talking to a guy with long, black, curly hair. The guy wore a black Led Zeppelin T-shirt and black leather gloves. He had tattoos on both arms and about a million bangles on his wrists and a medallion with a serpent on it around his neck. Apparently, he was finished talking with Bob Watson. He got up and punched some numbers into a cell phone and stalked toward the door. He seemed to be in a hurry. He passed by Brother John and me without acknowledging our presence.

"Hey, guys," Bob said.

"Was that one of the guys in Testimony?" I said.

Bob laughed. "That's a good one, Maddog. So how you feeling? You ready to lay some tracks?"

I didn't get the joke.

"I'm ready," I said. "But really, where's the rest of the band?"

"You'll get to meet them tomorrow. In the meantime, I got some solid drum tracks down this afternoon, so we can go ahead and lay some guitar on top of those."

"OK."

My Marshall stack was set up in the main room. There was a Steinway grand and a bunch of microphones on stands off to one side. Wood paneling, vaulted ceiling, recessed lights. You could have heard a pin drop in there.

"I'm going to be in the control room with Brother John and the engineer," Bob said. "Go ahead and get set up and get tuned and everything, and then just put those cans on when you're ready."

He gestured toward a set of headphones on the stool by my amp.

"OK," I said.

I tuned my guitar and plugged everything in. There was a cable connected from the Marshall head to a direct box in the wall, and there was a microphone positioned to pick up ambient sound from the speaker cabinets. I put the headphones on and sat on the stool.

"Can you hear me, Maddog?"

"Yes."

"I'm Roger Henley. I'm the engineer on the record. Tonight I want to get some rhythm guitar tracks for all ten songs. These are just dummy tracks for the vocals, so they don't have to be perfect."

"Where do you want to start?"

"Let's try 'Need to Know' first. You're going to hear four clicks, and then the drums will come in. Ready?"

"Go for it," I said.

I heard four clicks and then started playing chords along with the drums. It was easy. I knew all the songs by heart, and I didn't make any mistakes. We went through all the songs that I'd learned the same way. It was a little after ten when we finished the last song.

Bob Watson and Brother John and Roger Henley walked from the control room into the main room while I was stowing my gear. Bob introduced me to Roger and we shook hands.

"Anybody want to go over to Dillon's for a beer?" Bob said.

"I need to get going," Roger said. "But nice to meet you, Maddog. You did a great job, man."

"My pleasure," I said.

Roger left the studio.

"I'm a little tired myself," Brother John said. "I think Maddog and I should go on back and get a good night's sleep. We have another full day tomorrow."

"I wouldn't mind going for a beer," I said.

Bob said he would give me a ride back to the hotel. Brother John didn't seem very happy about it, but he finally said that would be OK. We took the elevator to the first floor and exited the building and parted ways across the street. Brother John headed toward his Mercedes in the parking lot, and Bob Watson and I walked over to Dillon's Irish Pub and Grill.

CHAPTER THIRTY-FIVE

There wasn't much of a crowd, but I reminded myself it was Tuesday and there naturally wouldn't be. The place was fairly big as far as pubs go, with booths and sitting areas and a regulation-size pool table. Wood and leather everywhere. There were maybe twenty stools around the horseshoe-shaped bar, and on one of them sat Ericka, the receptionist who had winked at me earlier. She was alone. I followed Bob to the bar. He took the stool next to Ericka, and I took the one next to him.

"Hi, guys," Ericka said.

"Hi, beautiful," Bob said. "Have you met my friend, Alexander Maddox?"

"I don't think we were ever introduced," she said.

I stood and offered my hand. "My friends call me Maddog. Or just Dog."

She giggled. "Maddog? Really? You don't look like a Maddog. But I guess everyone has to have a crazy nickname these days. Like what's-his-name who came in for a mastering session this afternoon."

"Slash," Bob said.

"Yeah, him. So why not just Alexander? It's a very nice name."

"You can call me Alexander if you want to," I said.

The young lady behind the bar wore a plaid skirt and a white knit shirt with the pub's logo over her left breast. She had olive skin and dark eyes and long, silky, black hair. She was very beautiful, maybe even more beautiful than Ericka. She came over and asked us what we wanted to drink.

"What do you have on draft?" Bob said.

She put her hands on her hips and stared at him. It was a joke. There were more brands on tap than I'd ever seen in one place. I counted thirty, and there were more on the other side of the bar.

Bob laughed. "Come on, Susan. I'll give you a hundred bucks if you can name every one of them without looking."

"Budweiser, Killian's, Newcastle, Stella Artois, Peroni..."

She kept going until she had named every one. Bob took a wad of cash out of his pocket and peeled off a hundred-dollar bill.

"Impressive," he said. "Here you go. You earned it."

She took the bill and stuffed it into a pocket on the inside of her skirt. "So what'll it be?"

"The usual," Bob said. "You can chuck the rest of that shit in the river."

Susan looked at me. I didn't know what the usual was, but I told her to make it two. She brought the beers and Bob paid for them. She took the money and said thank you and turned her attention to a couple on the other side of the bar.

Bob asked Ericka what she was doing out by herself on a Tuesday.

"My roommate's parents are in town this week," she said. "They're staying at the house, and I just figured I would make myself as scarce as possible. Her mom can be a pain in the ass."

We sipped our beers. Ericka was drinking something clear on ice with a lime in it.

Bob's cell phone trilled. He answered, and his expression turned sour when he listened to what the other party had to say. He disconnected and put the phone back in his pocket.

"I have to go," he said. "Sorry, Dog. I'll drop you at the hotel."

I didn't want to go. I wanted to talk with Ericka some more.

"I'll give him a ride," Ericka said.

"You sure?"

"I'm sure."

Bob looked at me.

"I would like to finish my beer," I said.

Bob said he would see me back in Studio B around ten in the morning and I said OK. He left the pub with a worried look on his face.

"So you have a place we can go?" Ericka said.

"A place we can go?"

She looked at the ice in her drink. "I'm not usually this forward."

"I'm staying at the Beverly Hills Hotel," I said.

"So you still want to finish that beer?"

"Maybe we could just grab a six-pack on the way."

We grabbed a six-pack on the way. We started kissing and tearing each other's clothes off as soon as we got in the room. We fell on the bed together and went at it for a long time and when we were finished, we lay there in a tight embrace while the ceiling fan hummed overhead.

"You want a beer?" I said.

"Yes. That sounds wonderful."

I got up and took two cans out of the mini refrigerator, opened them, and brought them to bed. We propped some pillows against the headboard and sat there sipping the cold beers. We didn't say anything for a few minutes. I felt what I had done was very wrong, but I didn't know why.

"So tell me all about Alexander Maddox," Ericka said.

"What do you mean?"

"You know, where you grew up, where you went to school, what kinds of bands you've been in, how many times you've been married, all that good stuff. Let's start with that tattoo on your arm. Where did you get that?"

"I don't know."

She looked at the ports on my PICC line, but didn't say anything. She leaned against my shoulder. "It's OK. You don't have to tell me anything you don't want to."

It wasn't that I didn't want to tell her those things. I genuinely didn't know. It was as if my past had been completely erased. It was gone, like pages torn from a book.

I got up and put my underwear on, opened the drapes, and looked out at the big rectangular swimming pool. It was after midnight and there was a guy out there swimming laps.

"What are you thinking?" Ericka said.

"Don't you know men hate it when you ask them that?"

"Why do they hate it? Is it because what they're thinking is a big profound secret, or because they're afraid to admit there's nothing more than football and pussy rattling around up there?"

"Probably the latter," I said.

"So what are you thinking?"

"Let's put it this way: I don't know anything about football."

"You want to make love some more?"

"I do, but…"

"But?"

"It's hard to explain. I feel guilty for some reason."

"You got a wife or a girlfriend or something?"

"Maybe. I don't know."

She got up and started putting her clothes on. "Musicians are so fucking weird," she said.

She grabbed her keys and walked out.

I didn't try to stop her.

I tossed and turned and finally gave up on trying to sleep. At six, I got dressed and went to the dining area for breakfast. I ate some eggs and toast and drank a few cups of coffee and read the newspaper and then went back to the room and watched television. A little before ten, Brother John drove me to the studio in his Mercedes. He dropped me at the curb, said he had some errands to run.

"I'll bring you guys some lunch after a while," he said.

"I need my shot."

He gave me the shot and I went inside and stopped at the desk to sign in. A skinny guy wearing a yellow shirt sat there typing something into the computer. His nametag said Brandon.

"Where's Ericka?" I said.

"Called in sick. You got some ID?"

"I'm meeting Bob Watson on the eighth floor. Studio B."

"You got some ID?"

"No. My name is Alexander Maddox. My friends call me Maddog. Or just Dog."

"I can't let you go upstairs without a picture ID. I'll have to call and get you an escort."

"OK."

I walked around the lobby and looked at some of the gold records while I waited. I was reading the stats on Grand Funk Railroad's *We're an American Band* when a framed photograph caught my eye. It was a band called Colt .45, and on the left side of the picture stood a very young man, twenty-four or twenty-five, with hair to his shoulders and a full beard. He wore bell-bottom jeans and a denim jacket with the sleeves cut off. He was holding a red hollow-body electric guitar, and there was a white bandana tied around his head.

I read the caption and a lifetime of memories started swirling through my head like a tornado.

CHAPTER THIRTY-SIX

It all came back to me in an instant. I remembered the way my mother smelled the final time she left for work, minutes before crashing into an oak tree and dying on the way to the hospital. I remembered the day my stepfather taught me how to use a bait-caster reel, and the day he stabbed me in the gut with a steak knife. I remembered my first guitar. First record deal. First trip to Jamaica, where I met my wife, Susan. I remembered going through the pregnancy with her and rubbing lotion on her feet and belly every night and being in the delivery room when our baby Harmony was born and cutting the cord. I remembered being the sole survivor of the plane crash that killed Susan and Harmony and everyone in my band. I remembered giving up on music and going through a very dark period and hitting rock bottom and finally deciding to study and get a private investigator's license. I remembered living in an Airstream camper on lot 23 at Joe's Fish Camp and the life-changing case three years ago when a young lady named Leitha Ryan hired me to find her fifteen-year-old sister Brittney who had run away from home.

One thing led to another and I ended up infiltrating a group of white supremacists called Chain of Light, led by a self-proclaimed prophet named Lucius Strychar. Strychar had been keeping a journal called The Holy Record for a lot of years about his experiences as a minister and his personal conversations with Jesus Christ, and I desperately wanted to get my hands on that book. But some strange things started happening. They tried to drug me and I escaped into the woods in a van. I had a hostage named Brother John and he had the angel tattoo on his arm and a burning cross tattoo on his chest and he was one of the most hateful racist motherfuckers I'd ever met and I tortured him into giving me information about...

Brother John. Was the guy I had tortured and pistol-whipped and left unconscious in the woods at the Chain of Light Ranch the same guy who had brainwashed me and brought me to California?

I got short of breath and my heart pounded in my temples and for a minute I felt like I might pass out.

I went to the restroom and splashed some cold water on my face. It wasn't him. The guy I was dealing with now didn't look anything like the Brother John at Chain of Light.

But he sounded like him.

Maybe he had gotten some plastic surgery or something to disguise himself. It would have been an extreme thing to do, but the Harvest Angels were an extreme group.

Thinking about them triggered another memory, one that I hoped was false. I pulled my shirt off and, sure enough, there it was. The angel tattoo. Brother John had tried to make me one of them, but why? Why me? Was all this part of some sort of elaborate scheme to exact revenge for the pain I had inflicted on him at Chain of Light?

And why did he bring me to California to record with the band Testimony? That especially didn't make sense. There had to be more to it.

Someone knocked on the restroom door.

"Mr. Maddox, your escort is here."

"Be out in a minute," I said.

I pulled some paper towels out of the dispenser and dried my hands and face and tried to figure out what to do next.

CHAPTER THIRTY-SEVEN

I was three thousand miles from home with no money and no way of proving my identity. I tried to think of what crimes Brother John had committed, but other than abducting me and drugging me and mind-fucking me, I couldn't think of any. If I went to the police it would be my word against his, and the tattoo on my arm would not work in my favor.

I figured Derek Wahl had been similarly kidnapped and brainwashed and that Brother John and company had been responsible for the Lamb murders, but I had no way to prove any of it. The only witnesses that might still be alive were Virgil Lamb and his grandson Joe, but I didn't think that was very likely. They were probably at the bottom of a lake or buried somewhere on the mountain.

I looked in the mirror at the tattoo on my left arm. Fine work. Amazing detail. I would do whatever it took to have it removed. If necessary, I would scrape it off myself with a cheese grater.

On the other side of my arm dangled the ports to my PICC line, which reminded me that even though I had my memory back I was still a drug addict.

As an upper-echelon musician, I had known a lot of guys who had done a lot of drugs. There were the guys like me, who stuck to weed and alcohol and the occasional snort of cocaine, and there were the guys who stuck needles in their arms. Smack. Chiba. Horse. Junk. Skag. Mud. Dope. Scat.

It all meant the same thing.

Heroin.

I knew guys, even guys in my own band, who functioned perfectly well on it for years. They would have a fix in the morning like most people have coffee, and they would go about their daily business. They would go to the bank, the post office, the grocery store. They would stop at Huddle House for a plate of sausage and eggs. They would come to rehearsal and smoke cigarettes and marijuana with the rest of us and maybe drink a beer and when we took a break, they would go off by themselves and shoot that shit into their arms.

Everything was hunky-dory until they couldn't get the drug for one reason or another. Then they became very sick individuals. Their brains needed the drug like a sponge needs water. Their entire existence depended on it. They would do whatever it took to get it. They would kill for it if they had to.

A drummer named Harley Krettak tried to borrow a thousand dollars from me one time. Colt .45 had just come off tour, and we'd gotten word that *Dead Ringer*, our third album, had gone platinum. I was flush with cash. I could have thrown Harley a grand with no problem. I never would have missed it. He said it was for rent and food, but I knew better. Harley was an addict. You could see it in his eyes, and you could see it on his arms. My thousand dollars wouldn't have helped him. He would have needed another thousand in a few days.

I said no. It wasn't about the money. I just didn't want to contribute to the cause when I knew the cause was an early grave.

Twenty-four hours after I turned him down for the loan, Harley Krettak walked into a convenience store with a sawed-off shotgun and told the clerk to open the safe. The clerk said she didn't know the combination, so Harley pulled the trigger and blew her face off. A friend in the sheriff's department let me watch the security video. The hatred in Harley's eyes made Charles Manson look like an altar boy.

Last I heard, Harley was still on death row in the Florida State Prison in Starke. Last I heard, it's hard to score dope there, and they don't let you have a drum set.

I thought about going to the police and having Brother John arrested for drug possession, but I figured that wouldn't work either. He had inserted a urinary catheter in me and a feeding tube and a PICC line. He was obviously a medical doctor, which meant he probably had a license to dispense narcotics. The drug he had turned me into a junkie with was probably not heroin off the street. It was probably a pharmaceutical analgesic called Dilaudid. I had taken it before in tablet form, but the intravenous version was much quicker and much more potent. It produced euphoric states similar to heroin's, and it was every bit as addictive.

I decided to go on up to the eighth floor and play along for a while until I could find a way to nail Brother John for something that would put him away for a long time. I put my shirt on and walked back out to the lobby. There was a petite woman in a business suit waiting at the elevator bank with a walkie-talkie.

"Hi, Mr. Maddox," she said.

"My friends call me Maddog. Or just Dog."

"OK, Dog. Ready to go up?"

"Absolutely."

We took the elevator to the eighth floor and she stayed with me until we reached the studio. Bob Watson was waiting at the entrance and he vouched for my identity. The petite woman said good-bye and marched back toward the elevators.

"Forget your wallet this morning?" Bob said.

"Yeah. Actually, I lost it. ID, credit cards, everything."

"That sucks. What a pain in the ass."

"You're not kidding."

He gestured toward the main room. "Come on back and meet the guys."

"OK."

Bob introduced me to Dan Powers, Jack Dixon, and Warren Boxx, Testimony's lead singer, bass player, and drummer.

"We're looking for a permanent guitar player," Dan said. "Think you might be interested?"

"Let's see how it goes with this record," I said.

"Cool. Bob and I would like to get you in the big room with Jack and Warren today, see if we can add some live energy to some of these tracks."

"OK."

There was a drum set and a bass rig already set up in the main room. I plugged into the Marshall and went through the songs with Jack and Warren. They were good musicians and we made it through all ten songs with no problem. I was on autopilot most of the time, trying to think of a way out of this mess and a way to send Brother John and his brainwashed brethren to prison.

A wall and a window separated the main room from the control room, and through the window we could see Bob and Dan and Roger working at the console. Throughout the session, they issued instructions through our headsets, and when we finished the last song Bob gave us a thumbs-up and told us to break for lunch.

We put our instruments away and walked to the control room. Roger sat at the thirty-six-channel mixing board and let us listen to the recording.

"It's sounding really good," Bob said. "What I'd like to do this afternoon is—"

The door opened and Brother John walked in carrying two large bags that said Chico's Mexican Food.

"Anybody hungry?" he said.

—〜〜—

After lunch the guys in Testimony left the studio and Bob worked with me on the lead solos to three of the songs. By four o'clock I was jonesing for another shot. I asked if we could take a break, and then I asked Brother John if I could speak to him in private. He grabbed his doctor bag and led me through a set of mirrored sliding glass doors and into a storage area behind the control room. I slid the door shut and latched the deadbolt.

"What's your name?" he said.

I hesitated for a second. I wanted that shot. I wanted it more than almost anything.

But while we were eating lunch something had clicked, something I might have thought about sooner if half my brain cells hadn't been saturated with the most powerful narcotic painkiller on the planet. When we met at Blue Water Bay on Fat Tuesday, Donna Wahl told me that the police had found some DNA at the Lambs' residence that didn't belong to any of the Lambs or to her brother, Derek. Allison Parker, the great-niece who was trying to sell the Lambs' house, said the DNA sample came from a bloody fingerprint on a piece of rubber. The police figured the murderer had worn a mask and that the mask had gotten torn in the scuffle, but if my hunch was correct, that's not what happened.

When I was first kidnapped and taken to the compound, I had started referring to Brother John as Stoneface. I called him that because his face lacked expression. He never smiled, never frowned, just looked pretty much the same all the time.

I didn't think much about it. Some people are just like that. But while we were eating, I noticed that something wasn't quite right. The food he'd brought was hot and spicy and the room was kind of warm, and everyone else's nose had an oily sheen while Brother John's was bone dry. That's when I put two and two together.

The guy had a plastic face. Or at least part of it was plastic.

I saw a man on television one time who had lost his nose and upper palate to cancer. He had a prosthesis he could snap on and off like a vacuum cleaner attachment. Damnedest thing I'd ever seen. I figured Brother John had something similar, and that part of it had gotten torn during the struggle at the Lambs' house. If that was the case, then the police already had all the evidence they would need to convict him of the murders.

Time for me to get the hell out of Dodge.

"What's your name?" Brother John repeated.

I clocked him in the jaw with an uppercut. His knees buckled and he fell to the floor.

I stood over him with clenched fists.

"Nicholas Colt, motherfucker. My name's Nicholas Colt."

CHAPTER THIRTY-EIGHT

I expected Brother John to get up and fight, or maybe even pull a weapon on me. He could have had a gun in his pocket for all I knew. My punch didn't knock him out, so I expected a fight. But he didn't get up. He stayed on the floor.

He worked the hinge of his jaw back and forth with his hand, and then looked up at me. "It doesn't matter," he said. "You're too late. The prophesy will be fulfilled."

"What are you talking about?"

"You'll see."

"I should stomp your fucking skull in right now," I said. "But I'm going to do the right thing. I'm going to hand you over to the police and hope you rot in prison."

"Haven't you done enough to me already?"

"I punched you in the jaw. Big fucking deal."

"Not that. What you did to me at Chain of Light."

"So it is you," I said.

"You probably think this is a disguise, but it's not. Three years ago at the Chain of Light Ranch, you tied me up in the back of a van and jammed a wooden pencil in my penis until I gave you the information you wanted. Then you knocked me unconscious with the butt of a pistol and left me in the woods. That was around midnight. By the time I woke up the next morning, my left eye and most of my face had been eaten by fire ants. Can you imagine the pain I went through? Can you even imagine?"

"You're lucky I didn't kill you then, and you're lucky I don't kill you now. Give me your phone."

He reached into his pocket, pulled out his cell phone, and tossed it to me. I called the police and identified myself and told them I was holding a murder suspect in a storage room on the eighth floor of the Capitol tower. The dispatcher promised help would be there shortly. She told me to stay on the line until the officers arrived, but I had another call to make. I disconnected and punched in Juliet's number.

"Hello?"

"It's me."

"Nicholas! Oh my God, we were so worried. I thought—"

"It's OK," I said. "I'm fine. It's over, Jules. Everything's going to be all right now. It's safe for you and Brittney to come home."

"Where are you?"

"Los Angeles. Long story."

"We'll catch a flight out as soon as we can," she said. "We have storm warnings here, so it might be a couple of days. Oh my God. I can't believe this. We'll have a layover at LAX, so maybe you can meet us there."

"I need to go to Tennessee," I said, "but I'll be in Florida by the time you guys get home."

"Oh, Nicholas, I'm so excited. Every day I prayed that you were OK."

"Well, I am. Is Brittney nearby?"

She said that Brittney was out swimming in the ocean. Naturally, Juliet wanted to know about everything that had happened to me. I told her I would fill her in later. I told her I loved her and that I would see her soon.

Ten minutes later, someone banged on the door. I unlatched the deadbolt, and two uniformed officers stepped into the room. One of them was named Peterson, the other Garcia.

"What's this all about?" Garcia said.

"It's about murder," I said. "The piece of shit on the floor here killed at least two people, probably more. He kidnapped me and drugged me and brainwashed me, and he did the same to an officer named Derek Wahl in Tennessee." I told them everything, from the beginning, and I showed them the tattoo on my arm and the PICC line. I told them the evidence to convict Brother John was at the state police post in Mont Falcon.

When I finished talking, Brother John said, "I want to speak to my lawyer."

"You're not denying the accusations?" Peterson said.

"I want to speak to my lawyer."

Peterson said I would need to come to the station and give my statement to one of the homicide detectives, and I said I didn't have a problem with that.

Garcia cuffed Brother John and read him his rights, and they marched him out of the studio and toward the elevators. I was holding up the rear.

Bob Watson watched incredulously as we walked by.

—∞—

I had been waiting for almost two hours in an interrogation room at the substation when a guy wearing a white shirt and a necktie with a picture of Rocky Balboa on it walked in and identified himself as Detective Gregory Sloan. I looked at the tie. Only in Hollywood, I thought. He talked to me for a while with a tape recorder running and gave me some papers to fill out. I told him about Brother John's drivers back at the Beverly Hills Hotel and he said he would have them brought in for questioning. I asked him if he could help me get a duplicate driver's license and some money from my Florida bank account.

"I'll see what I can do," he said. "Just so you know, John Martin, the man you knew as Brother John, is going to be extradited to Tennessee immediately. His lawyer insisted on it, and we really have no reason to keep him here."

"He's a murderer," I said.

"He's an alleged murderer in Tennessee. That's where the crimes took place, and that's where the trial will be. He hasn't broken any laws in California. None that we know of. He'll be on a flight to Nashville with an armed escort early tomorrow morning."

Garcia and Peterson gave me a ride to the hotel. I took a shower and put on a fresh set of clothes, walked out to the road, and hitched a ride to the Hollywood Presbyterian Medical Center. I went through a set of doors under the big EMERGENCY sign and stopped at the admitting desk. The clerk's name was Betty.

"I need to see a doctor," I said.

"Could you tell me the nature of your problem this evening?"

"I'm having chest pain."

She didn't bat an eye. "Can I see your insurance card?"

"I don't have any."

"Picture ID?"

"Nope."

She sighed exasperatedly and asked me for my date of birth and my social security number and she gave me a long medical history form to fill out. Rule #110 in Nicholas Colt's *Philosophy of Life*: Never have a heart attack without your wallet on you.

I filled out the form and waited for a while. A young lady wearing pink scrubs called my name and led me to a room with several beds and partitioned by green drapes. She handed me a gown and told me to take my shirt off and lie on the bed. She took my blood pressure and temperature and asked me about the nature of my pain and how long I'd been having it. She gave me an aspirin and taped a nitroglycerine patch on my chest. She said the doctor would be in to see me shortly, and then another young lady wearing blue scrubs wheeled a machine in and put a bunch of wires on my chest. It was an EKG, she said, to let them know what was going on with my heart.

By the time the doctor came in, I was ready to strangle someone. Her nametag said K. Salloum, MD. She looked to be about Brittney's age. She listened to my chest with her stethoscope and examined the PICC line site.

"Where is your pain?" she said.

I pointed toward my sternum. "Here."

"And is it a sharp pain, a heaviness, a pressure—"

"More of a pressure," I said.

"And how long has this been going on?"

"Couple days. It's hurting really bad right now."

"On a scale of zero to ten?"

"Ten," I said.

"Why do you have the PICC line?"

"I had an infection. They sent me home with IV antibiotics."

Being married to a nurse has its advantages. I was giving Dr. Salloum all the right answers.

"Your EKG looks fine," she said. "I'm going to order some blood work and a stress test. We'll need to admit you for twenty-four-hour observation."

"Can I have something for the pain?"

"Are you allergic to any medications?"

"None that I know of."

"I'll have the nurse bring you something."

She walked away. A glacial age later, Pink Scrubs came back with two syringes in her hand.

"This is morphine," she said. She uncapped the port on my PICC line and administered the medication. It wasn't as good as the stuff Brother John had been giving me, but it took the edge off. When she left, I wadded some tape on the end of a tongue depressor and stuck the contraption into the sharps container and fished out the syringes she had discarded. I untied the gown, put my shirt back on, and nonchalantly walked out of the ER and out to the street where I proceeded to vomit in the gutter.

CHAPTER THIRTY-NINE

It took a while to sort everything out, but Detective Sloan had pulled some strings for me and three days later a FedEx envelope containing my driver's license and debit card was delivered to the hotel. I'd been charging meals to the room, and I had managed to talk a maid into letting me into the adjoining suite, where I found half a dozen vials of Dilaudid in a drawer. The Dilaudid had kept me going, but it was gone and I didn't want to go to a hospital again where they would probably give me morphine again and I would probably puke my guts up again.

I checked my balance at the ATM machine in the lobby. There was almost a thousand dollars in the account. I withdrew four hundred in cash, went back to my room, and packed a change of clothes and some toiletries into a carry-on bag. I took a taxi to Walmart and bought a prepaid cell phone and a sandwich at Subway. While I ate, I called some people and texted some others so they would have the new number. From there I took another taxi to the airport and bought a ticket for the red-eye to Nashville. It was a five-hour flight and I slept most of the way. I rented a car and got a motel room and tried to sleep some more but the bugs were all over me inside and out and I couldn't stand it. I drove to the bus station and hung out in the men's room for a while and sure enough, a guy with a backpack and an Afro and some gold teeth eventually walked in and recognized a potential customer when he saw one. He held out his palm and gently unfolded the corners of a foil packet.

"How much?" I said.

"Twenty."

"Give me five of them."

He unzipped his backpack and loaded five of the packets into a Ziploc bag. I handed him the money and he handed me the dope.

"Know where I can get a piece?" I said.

"You mean a gun?"

"Yeah."

"What you looking for?"

"Something I can put in my pocket."

He reached into the backpack and pulled out a small semiautomatic pistol with fake wooden grips. I recognized it right away. It was a Raven Arms MP-25, one of the cheapest handguns ever produced, what we commonly refer to as a Saturday night special. Under normal circumstances, I would have told him to stick that thing up his ass.

"How much you want for it?" I said.

"Hundred bucks."

"I'll give you fifty."

"Seventy-five."

"You got some shells to go with it?"

He pulled out a small box of .25-caliber cartridges. I gave him the seventy-five. On the way back to the motel, I stopped at a dollar store and bought some candles and a lighter and a cheap set of silverware. I knew you could get in trouble carrying a spoon around, that it could be considered drug paraphernalia, but I wasn't about to cut a Coke can in half like the street hypes do. I sat at the desk in the motel room and bent one of the spoons from the silverware set and lit one of the candles and unwrapped one of the foil packets. It was black tar heroin from Mexico. It looked exactly like the stuff you put on a roof. I scraped some off with the spoon, added some water to it, and cooked it over the candle. I drew it into one of the syringes I had stolen and injected it into my PICC line. I fell asleep in the chair and woke up a couple of hours later with a line of drool on my chin.

I didn't feel too chipper, but I felt like I could function. I drove my Ford Focus rental car to Pete Strong's house and called Juliet while I waited in the driveway.

"We're leaving tomorrow," she said. "Our flight is at eight fifteen tomorrow night, and we'll land in LA at around eleven Friday morning. Eleven eastern standard time, that is. It'll probably be five or six by the time we make it to Florida."

"That's a long flight."

"I know. And there's a long layover in Los Angeles. Over an hour."

"I should be home before you guys," I said. "I'll pick you up at the airport and we'll go out and celebrate."

"Oh, Nicholas. I can't wait to see you."

"Can't wait to see you, babe. Can I talk to Brittney for a minute?"

"Sure. Hold on."

Someone tried to call while I was waiting for Brittney to come to the phone. I let it go to voice mail.

"Daddy!"

"Hi, sweetheart."

"Oh my God, we thought you were dead or something. What happened?"

"It's a long, long story. I'll tell you about it when we get home."

"Was that Derek guy who broke into the house and cut us with the Harvest Angels?"

"He was, but I think he was kidnapped and brainwashed. I don't think he joined of his own volition."

"Why does your voice sound funny?"

"Does it?"

"Yeah. Are you drunk?"

"Just tired, I guess. You keeping up with your schoolwork?"

While she was telling me about her paper for English, Denise pulled into the driveway and parked beside me. Our eyes met through the car windows, and she gave me a little smile. It was obvious she had been crying.

"And I met this really cool guy here," Brittney said. "His name's Rey, and he's an awesome basketball player."

"They play basketball in the Philippines?"

She laughed. "Of course they do. They have indoor plumbing and everything."

"Huh. I pictured it to be something like *Gilligan's Island*."

She laughed again. Sometimes I forced her to watch reruns with me. That's the only reason she even knew what I was talking about.

"Dad, you would love it here. I swear, it's beautiful."

"Guess I'll have to go sometime."

"Yeah! Maybe we could all take a vacation here this summer after graduation. That would be sweet."

"Maybe. Listen, someone here's waiting to talk to me, so I need to go. I'll see you guys in a couple of days."

"Love you, Daddy."

"I love you, too."

I had talked to Denise before I left LA. The local authorities had raided Brother John's compound in the middle of the night.

They arrested everyone and confiscated a huge cache of weapons and explosives. Now they faced the daunting task of sorting through the members and determining which ones were there by choice and which ones had been abducted and brainwashed, like me. They found Pete's body in a shallow grave not far from the tree he'd been hanged from.

I got out of the car and gave Denise a hug.

"I wanted to give you this," I said.

I handed her Pete's Rolex, and she burst into tears. I hugged her some more.

"Come on in," she said. "I'll make some coffee."

We walked inside and I followed Denise to the kitchen. I sat at the table while she scooped some Hills Bros. into the filter basket and poured some water into the reservoir. She came over and sat across from me while it brewed.

"We tried to find you guys," she said. "We tried so hard. I had every one of our investigators working on it twenty-four-seven."

"I know you tried. Don't blame yourself."

"Some of my friends think I should blame *you*, for getting Pete involved in the first place."

"Do you?"

"No. Pete did what he wanted to do. I tried to talk him out of it, but he was convinced it was the right thing."

"I'm so sorry it turned out the way it did."

"I had him cremated today. That's what he wanted. The memorial service is tomorrow at four."

"I'll be there," I said.

The coffee pot started gurgling and Denise got up and poured us each a cup. She asked if I wanted cream and sugar, then remembered from the restaurant that I took it black. She sat back down and we sipped in silence for a couple of minutes. The coffee was very good.

"They found Virgil Lamb," she said.

"Alive?"

"Barely. But yes, he's in the ICU over at General."

"What about Joe, his grandson?"

"Buried not far from where they found Pete."

"Damn. I wonder if it would be possible for me to talk to Virgil?"

"Why would you want to now?"

"Just a few things I'd like to get straight. Like how Brother John was able to enter Virgil's house on Thanksgiving Day, butcher his wife and daughter-in-law, and kidnap him and Joe and Derek Wahl, and walk out practically unscathed. I'd like to know how, and I'd like to know why."

Denise looked thoughtfully at the steaming black liquid in her cup. "You know Ted Grayson's under investigation, right?"

"I implicated him in the report I filed in LA. I figured he set me up. I also told them about Garland what's-his-name, the state trooper who drove me back to the compound after I escaped."

"Garland Yokum. They arrested him."

"Good. I hope this puts an end to the Harvest Angels."

"That was your goal from the beginning, and it looks like you succeeded."

"Everything comes with a price, though. This time it was your husband. I want you to know he won't be forgotten."

"Can I get you some more coffee?"

"Thanks, but I need to get going."

I got up and she walked me to the door. We embraced, longer and tighter than necessary. It wasn't the embrace of a friend consoling a friend. It was the embrace of a man and a woman who wanted each other, who needed each other.

"I don't want to be alone tonight," she said.

"Denise—"

"I know you're married. I know. All I'm asking for is one night."

She was a very beautiful woman. Smart and sexy, with a passion for life you don't see every day. All she was asking for was one night, but it never ends up that way. One night turns into two, and two into three. Lives are wrecked and hearts are broken, all because of a chemical reaction in the brain that compels attraction. Technically, I'd already cheated on my wife once during this excursion, in Hollywood with Ericka, the receptionist. But I wasn't myself at the time. At the time, I didn't even know I had a wife. There was no need for Juliet to know about that. Ever. It was meaningless, and it would only hurt her to know. With Denise, though, I had a feeling it wouldn't be meaningless. I had a feeling that if I stayed with her for one night, I might never leave.

"I'm sorry," I said.

I turned and took a deep breath and walked out the door and didn't look back.

CHAPTER FORTY

I needed a shot. I wondered if that was part of the reason I'd walked away from Denise with such little hesitation. What I really wanted was back at the motel. I was starting to second-guess my own motivations, my scruples, and my sanity.

Before leaving the driveway, I checked the voice mail that had come in while I was talking to Brittney. It was from a state police detective in Mont Falcon named Rex Atbury. He told me to give him a call, so I did.

"I got your number from Greg Sloan out in Hollywood," he said. "We extradited John Martin, and we'd like for you to come to the station here in Mont Falcon and help us fill out the report."

"You want me to come now?"

"First thing in the morning, if you could. Around eight?"

"All right," I said. "I'll be there."

I decided to drive on down and spend the night in Mont Falcon. It would put me that much closer to Florida, and I wouldn't have to fight the morning traffic in Nashville. I'd promised Denise that I would be at Pete's memorial service, but I thought it might be awkward now after our scene at the door. I decided it would be best if I never saw Denise Strong again.

On the way back to the motel, I passed Nashville General Hospital and I remembered what Denise had said, that Virgil Lamb was a patient there in the Intensive Care Unit. I made a U-turn and pulled into the visitors' parking area.

I was badly in need of a fix, but I figured this might be my only chance to meet Virgil and get some information from him. I walked into the main entrance, followed the signs, took an elevator to the sixth floor. I followed some more signs and navigated a confusing labyrinth that finally led me to the ICU nurses' station. I talked to a clerk at the desk.

"I'm looking for a patient named Virgil Lamb," I said.

She looked on her computer screen. "You know he's a police hold, right?"

"I just want to talk to him for a few minutes."

"Prisoners aren't allowed to have visitors. Sorry."

"Can I talk to his nurse?"

She tapped a fingernail on a touch screen, picked up a telephone receiver and said, "Sharon, there's someone at the desk who would like to speak with you."

I stood there and examined the design on the floor tiles while I waited. My hands were in my pockets to keep them from trembling. Doctors and nurses scurried to and fro with a sense of urgency. They talked to each other over binders and clipboards, and there was a vibe that what they were doing really mattered. And it did, of course. They literally held people's lives in their hands. I wondered if I could deal with that kind of stress on a daily basis. I didn't think so.

A tall slender woman wearing blue scrubs and a stethoscope and Crocs came and shook my hand and introduced herself as Sharon.

"What's his condition?" I asked.

"Are you family?"

"I'm his son," I lied. "Just came up from Florida."

"He's comatose," Sharon said. "On a ventilator. I hate to be the one to tell you this, but we're really not expecting him to pull through."

"What happened?"

"He was in that compound they raided down by Black Creek. Some kind of cult. I'm sure you heard about it on the news."

"Yeah. I know about that. But why is he in a coma?"

"They found him in a room by himself, strapped into a dentist's chair. He was emaciated. He'd been tortured and given all sorts of drugs. The cops are still trying to sort it all out."

"My God," I said, trying to sound astonished. "If I leave my number, will you be sure to contact me if there's any change in his condition?"

"Sure. I'm really sorry we can't let you in to see him. Sheriff's department regulations."

"I understand."

I wrote my cell number on a piece of paper and she took it and put it on Virgil's chart.

—∞—

When I got back to the motel, I cooked another dose of smack and injected it into my PICC line. There were only three of the foil packets left. I thought about calling the guy from the bus station and scoring some more before leaving Nashville, but I figured it wouldn't be that hard to find elsewhere. Especially the black tar shit. In certain parts of Jacksonville, there's a dealer on every corner. It's like going through the drive-through at Burger King. You don't even have to get out of your car.

I packed my things and checked out and took the interstate south to Mont Falcon. It was only fifty miles, but I almost nodded off a couple of times on the way down. I stopped at a gas station and bought coffee and a Kit Kat bar and wished I'd chosen Butterfinger or something because I couldn't get the stupid little jingle out of my head. *Gimme a break, gimme a break…*

The Mont Falcon motel looked a lot different in the springtime. There were flowers blooming, butterflies flittering, and crape myrtles towering past the eaves. Moe's Ribs had a new paint job and a new sign, and the cool mountain air was rich with the scents of jasmine and barbecued meat.

Beulah was sitting in her chair at the front desk. When I walked in she got up, stood at the computer, and asked if she could help me.

"It's me," I said. "Nicholas Colt."

"Oh!" She came out from behind the desk and gave me a hug. "I didn't recognize you without the beard. And your hair's a lot shorter. I heard your name on the news the other day and I said, 'Hey, I know him.' What an exciting time you've had!"

"Exciting's not the word for it."

"Are you heading back to Florida?"

"Yeah. I'm only here for one night."

She went back to her computer. "You want your old room back? It's available."

"Sure," I said.

I handed her my debit card and she swiped it and gave it back to me along with the room key. She said to come back to the office and chat after a while if I could, and I said I would try. I walked to the room and opened the door and was pleasantly surprised to see that the walls had been painted and that new carpeting had been put down. Gone was the smell of stale tobacco smoke, and the framed print of ducks flying over a pond had been replaced with a copy of Van Gogh's *Sunflowers*. I was impressed. I opened the door and looked and there was one of those red circles with a line through it over a picture of a cigarette. I hadn't noticed it on the way in.

I even had a signal on my cell phone. They must have finally put that tower up.

I took my shoes off and got on the bed and leaned against the headboard and switched on the television. I watched CNN for a while and part of a baseball game, and then I remembered it had been quite a while since I'd eaten. I didn't particularly want to go to Moe's Ribs, but it was the only restaurant in the vicinity and it wouldn't have been practical to get groceries since I was leaving the next morning. I put my shoes back on and walked over there and sat at a booth. A pretty, young waitress named Kelly brought me a glass of water with a lemon wedge in it and gave me a menu to look at but I already knew what I wanted. I ordered a full rack of ribs and a baked potato and salad. There were some pies on display in a glass case on the counter, and I was already thinking about a slice of apple with a scoop of vanilla ice cream on top for dessert.

After dinner I went back to the room and gave myself a shot and fell asleep watching *Wheel of Fortune*.

And for the first time in forty years, I dreamed about The Potato Man.

CHAPTER FORTY-ONE

When I was seven or eight years old, I started having recurring nightmares featuring a potato with a face and arms and legs. The Potato Man. He had big, horselike teeth and would chase me all over the house. I was scared to death of him. One of my friends was in my dream one time and he caught The Potato Man and tried to squeeze the life out of him, but The Potato Man bit my friend in the palm of his hand and my friend said the bite burned like fire.

The Potato Man would always tell me something, some bit of profound knowledge that I couldn't remember when I woke up. That was the strangest part of it all. Here was this lightning-quick, devilish tuber with acid for saliva, and in the end he turned out to be some sort of ethereal soothsayer.

I woke up sweating in the motel bed, and just like when I was a kid, The Potato Man had told me something extremely important that I couldn't remember.

I switched the television off and got up and took a shower and put my one fresh change of clothes on and stepped out into the misty dawn. I wanted to get my meeting with the police detective over with so I could start the nine-hour drive home. I only had two foil packets left, but I figured they would last me until evening when I could find a dealer in Jacksonville. In a pinch I could always prowl around Atlanta for a while, but I didn't think I would need to.

The state police substation was just outside of town. I got there a few minutes before eight. The desk sergeant escorted me down a long hallway to a door that said HOMICIDE. Rex Atbury sat at an oak desk scarred with cigarette burns and coffee rings.

"Come on in," Atbury said.

The sergeant left and closed the door. Atbury motioned for me to have a seat.

"Hope I'm not too early," I said.

"Early is good. I like early. You want some coffee?"

"I had a cup on the way over. But thanks."

He opened a notebook and took a pencil from a blue ceramic caddy on the desk. "This shouldn't take long," he said. "I just wanted to go over a few things with you."

"OK."

"How long have you known John Martin?"

"I first encountered him three years ago down in Florida. He was part of a neo-Nazi cult called the Chain of Light. Their militant branch was called the Harvest Angels, and he was part of that. I was instrumental in shutting the whole deal down. A bunch of people were arrested, but Brother John slipped through somehow."

"So how did you manage to run into him again in Tennessee?"

"An old girlfriend in Florida met me for dinner one night and told me her brother had been missing for over a year. Her brother was Derek Wahl. She wanted me to come up here and take a look around, but I'd allowed my PI license to go inactive and I didn't really have any interest in the case until she told me about the slanted crucifixes carved into the victims' foreheads."

"The murders at the Lambs' place," Atbury said.

"Right. A client of mine in Florida was killed and marked with the same kind of wound. The perpetrator turned out to be a member of the Harvest Angels, so I figured the tilted cross thing might be some kind of calling card. That's why I came up here. I did some legwork and talked to some people and decided the murders were probably a copycat, but when I got home Derek Wahl was there about to kill my wife and daughter. He cut crosses in their foreheads, so that's when I knew—"

"That Derek was part of the cult."

"Yes. But now I think he was probably brainwashed, like I was."

"What makes you think that?"

"He was a cop. He was called to the Lambs' residence for a domestic disturbance. That's when he went missing. Brother John kidnapped him and brainwashed him and sent him to Florida to kill my family."

"How do you know Derek wasn't in on the whole thing?"

"The nine-one-one call is on record. Somebody made the call, the dispatcher sent Derek to the house, and—"

"Derek was the only cop on duty in Black Creek that day," Atbury said. "Think about it. He could have had someone make the nine-one-one call, or he could have made it himself from a prepaid cell phone."

"I guess it could have happened like that."

"And don't you think it's just an incredible coincidence that you were drawn into it the way you were? Your ex-girlfriend just happened to have a brother who just happened to belong to a new cell of the cult you shut down three years ago and the leader of that cell just happened to be the man you tortured and left for dead in the woods, the man who blames you for his face being devoured by fire ants?"

"Are you saying I was set up?"

"I don't see any other way it could have gone down like it did. It had to have been planned from the get-go."

I was about to ask him who could have played me like that when it hit me like a ton of crab nachos.

CHAPTER FORTY-TWO

I drove back to the motel and loaded my things into the Ford Focus. I walked into the room for one last look around when my cell phone rang. I picked up.

"Hello."

"Is this Mr. Lamb?"

I recognized the voice. It was Sharon, the ICU nurse. I'd told her that I was Virgil Lamb's son.

"Yes," I said. "This is Nicholas Lamb."

"I'm breaking all kinds of rules here, and I'll get fired if anyone finds out, but your dad regained consciousness a while ago and I thought you might like to talk to him. His heart rate is in the forties and he's not breathing well, so this might be the last chance you'll have."

"Can you put him on now?"

"I will, but let me tell you, he's a bit confused. He keeps saying crazy things about how the world's going to end today. Sometimes it helps to talk to a family member."

"I'll see what I can do."

"OK, here he is."

The next voice I heard was a gravelly whisper. Even with the volume on the phone turned all the way up, I had to make a concerted effort to understand what he was saying.

"I know who you are," he said. "And I'm not confused."

"Who am I?"

"Nicholas Colt. You're a private investigator."

"That's right. How do you know that?"

"I was a prisoner at Brother John's complex, same as you. He forced me to tell him things."

"What kind of things?" I said.

"Things about my past, things that will happen in the future."

"You were a psychic in a traveling carnival. I know about that. But you don't expect me to believe—"

"Believe whatever you want to believe. I predicted the Japanese attack on Pearl Harbor. I predicted the Martin Luther King assassination and both Kennedy assassinations. I predicted the terrorist attack on the World Trade Center on nine-eleven. Just to name a few. None of those things had to happen. They could have been prevented if anyone had taken me seriously. The things I see are parts of one possible future, but the future can be changed. It happens every day."

"So you're saying that the world is going to end today?"

"The beginning of the end might happen today, but there's still time to stop it. There's still time if you'll only listen to me."

"How do you know all these things?" I said. "Is it like the voice of God speaks to you or something?"

"I just know. That's all."

I didn't believe a word of it, but I decided to humor him.

"OK," I said. "Let's just say all that's true. Why did Brother John come to your house and murder your wife and daughter-in-law? Why did he kidnap you and take you to his compound?"

I paused. I wondered why Virgil didn't predict *those* things. I wondered why he didn't predict them, and then try to prevent them. That's where the whole "psychic" thing falls apart for me. They're all full of shit. I let it go.

"And whatever happened to your grandson Joe?" I said.

"Brother John used my wife and daughter-in-law to lure you in. That's what that was all about. It was a trick. He knew that Roy Massengill had cut a tilted cross into Leitha Ryan's forehead, and he knew you were emotionally involved in that case. He knew duplicating that would draw you to Tennessee. He kidnapped me and Joe and brought us to his compound for one reason: he wanted me to tell him things to come. My grandson was only important in that he was important to me. Brother John made me watch Joe being tortured with electrical current. That's how he got me to tell him things. Joe was suffering so much, I begged Brother John to kill him. I promised to give him the ultimate prediction in return."

"What do you consider the ultimate prediction?"

"The day Jesus Christ will return to Earth. That's the one he wanted all along."

I dredged up a faint memory from Sunday school when I was a kid, before my mother's '65 Falcon slammed into an oak tree and nobody took me to church anymore. "Doesn't the Bible say that nobody knows when Christ will return?" I said.

"Yes. Matthew, chapter twenty-four, verse thirty-six: 'But of that day and hour knoweth no man, no, not the angels of Heaven, but my Father only.'"

"Seems pretty cut and dried."

"The angels of heaven don't know," he said. "But the angels of hell do."

"I see. So you told him the date that Christ is coming?"

"Yes. Unfortunately, it's a long way off and we'll be dead and gone by the time it happens. But, I also gave him the date of an event that will set the wheels in motion. That's the date we can do something about."

"And what date is that?"

"Today."

"And what's the event?" I said.

"There's going to be a nuclear explosion in Los Angeles."

His voice had gotten even weaker, and I could barely understand him.

"Did you say a nuclear explosion?" I said. "In Los Angeles?"

"Yes. You know those Marshall speaker cabinets you took to LA?"

"Yeah. As far as I know, they're still on the eighth floor of the Capitol tower. What about them?"

"In each of those speaker cabinets there's a small nuclear device commonly referred to as a suitcase bomb. Each bomb has a digital timer set for noon today. Eastern standard time. At that time, several square blocks of downtown Los Angeles will be vaporized."

"That's insane," I said. "Why would Brother John want to kill all those people?"

"Because I told him it was going to happen. In his mind, the prophesy must be fulfilled."

I tried to wrap my head around the sheer absurdity of it all. "Why Los Angeles?" I said.

"It's a densely populated area, for one. More bang for the buck. But it's more than that. Brother John's goal isn't simply to kill a hundred thousand or so people. The prophesy calls for something much more catastrophic."

I thought about it for a few seconds. The San Andreas Fault. That had to be it.

"He's hoping to cause an earthquake?" I said.

"Not just any earthquake. *The* earthquake. This one is going to send half of California reeling into the Pacific. And he's not just hoping to cause it. He showed me the graphs. By his calculations, the precise placement of the device combined with the strength of the blast will make a seismic event of epic proportions a mathematical certainty. There *will* be an earthquake, and it will kill millions of people."

"So that was the deal with me going in to record with that band? To get the bombs in?"

"Yes. And that's where the precise placement comes in. The Capitol Records building in downtown LA is in the optimal location to trigger the quake."

I was still puzzled as to why Brother John had concocted such an elaborate scheme. "Why not just park the van by the building and leave it there?" I said. "I don't see why he went through all that rigmarole."

"He needed time to get far away from California before the blast. If he'd parked the van and abandoned it, all kinds of things could have gone wrong."

"Like what?"

"People get nervous when they see an abandoned vehicle. They call the cops. The cops bring bomb-sniffing dogs, and then the bomb squad comes. On the other hand, nobody's going to suspect a world-class guitarist to be carrying a nuclear explosive in his speaker cabinets."

"So what's the point in killing all those people?" I said. "I still don't get it."

"Brother John had an envelope he planned to send to the director of Homeland Security. The nuclear devices in the Marshall speaker cabinets were originally built by the Soviet Union during the cold war. More recently, they were acquired by a country in the Middle East that…how should I put it…has historically had a rather strained relationship with the United States. In the envelope is a metal plate with a serial number on it, along with a note spelling everything out. The metal plate can easily be traced. Once our government discovers who was responsible for blowing California off the map, they will naturally retaliate. Do you think they're going to combat a nuclear strike with conventional weapons? Highly unlikely. It's going to be no-holds-barred this time. Despite protests from the rest of the world, the United States will be forced to launch a full-scale nuclear attack against—"

"You're talking about World War Three," I said. "If the United States starts firing nukes, then a bunch of other countries are going to get involved."

"Precisely," he said. "Today's mushroom cloud in LA is merely the catalyst, the first in a series of events that will lead to the end of the world as we know it."

It all made perfect sense. Brother John was going to facilitate the return of Jesus Christ by starting World War Three. In his mind, he was going to be a hero.

"And you're sure all this is going to happen?" I said.

"No. Like I said, it's one possible future. It can be changed. The people here won't listen to me. The guards, doctors, nurses, none of them. They think I'm a crazy old man, out of my mind. I'm a prisoner and they won't let me make phone calls. Otherwise, I would call in a bomb threat so the right people could get out there and defuse those things. It's up to you, Nicholas Colt. You need to make that call."

I wondered why Virgil was a prisoner, and then I remembered that the police were still sorting through the people found at Brother John's complex and determining which ones were there by choice and which ones had been abducted and brainwashed. Virgil obviously hadn't been cleared yet.

And something else clicked. Now I knew why Brother John didn't put up a fight when I punched him in the storage room at the Capitol Records building. He wanted to be taken into custody as quickly as possible, and extradited to Tennessee as quickly as possible. He didn't want to stay in LA and be vaporized by his own bombs.

I looked at the time on my cell phone. It was 9:37.

"All right," I said. "I'll make the call. I've been dealing with an LAPD detective. I'll call him directly and tell him everything you said. If you're lying—"

I heard a loud clank followed by what sounded like rubber-soled shoes squeaking on a tile floor. Someone said, *He's not breathing*, and then another voice shouted, *Call the code*. The phone went dead, and I had a strong feeling Virgil Lamb did, too.

I pulled Greg Sloan's business card out of my pocket and started punching in the number. I was about to hit the last digit when a freight train named Earl plowed into me and knocked me on the floor.

CHAPTER FORTY-THREE

Earl straddled me and pinned my wrists to the floor. He had hit me from behind and the impact had jarred the cell phone from my hand. It was only three feet away, but it might as well have been three miles.

Lester was walking around the room looking in drawers, but I'd already loaded everything into the car. All that was left was a Gideon's Bible and a phone directory.

"I don't care what you do to me," I said. "But I need to make a phone call, and I need to make it now."

"The only thing you need to do is shut the fuck up," Lester said.

"You don't understand. If I don't make that call, it might literally be the end of the world."

He laughed. "Yeah, right. It's fixin' to be the end of the world for you anyway, scout."

When Virgil Lamb told me there was going to be a nuclear explosion at twelve noon eastern standard time in the city of Los Angeles, the first thing I thought about was my wife and daughter. Juliet had told me their plane was landing at 11:00 a.m. (EST), and that they would be stuck at LAX for over an hour. If the bomb went off at twelve noon, Juliet and Brittney would be among those killed in the blast.

Lester sat at the desk and lit a joint. His lip was badly scarred from when I'd yanked the ring out of it. The upper lip and bottom lip didn't make a tight seal anymore, and he occasionally had to wipe the slobber from his chin. I had a feeling he probably had trouble getting dates now.

"Gimme a hit on that," Earl said.

Lester held the joint to Earl's mouth and he sucked on it and inhaled deeply and held the smoke in his lungs until his face turned blue. He finally coughed it out, inadvertently spraying me in the face with his vile spittle.

"This is a nonsmoking room," I said. "Didn't you see the sign?"

"Oh fucking well," Lester said, flicking ashes on the new carpet. "Rules were made to be broken. And so were fingers."

He got up and stomped my left hand with the heel of his work boot. There was a sickening series of cracks, and the pain shot through me like a lightning bolt. My hand started throbbing immediately. I couldn't see it, but I could feel the heat and the swelling. I shouted and said, *Motherfucker*. Tears trickled from the corners of my eyes, and at that moment, I knew I would never be able to play the guitar again.

"You're going to die, you son of a bitch," I said.

He took a hit on the joint. "You know, I can't drink from a straw anymore. My lips just don't fit together right. You took that simple pleasure from me, and now I'm going to take some things from you. One by one, slowly but surely, I'm going to take them. What goes around comes around. Ever heard that?"

I didn't say anything. I strained and bucked but Earl was too heavy to budge. The digital clock on the nightstand said 9:48. I was thinking there was still plenty of time if I could only make that call, and then I remembered that this part of Tennessee was on central time, so it was really an hour later. In my mind, I adjusted the clock to eastern standard time. It was really 10:48, which meant there was only a little over an hour until doomsday. Even if I had been able to call Detective Greg Sloan that second, I doubted the bomb squad would make it to the Capitol tower in time to defuse the explosives.

Lester reached into his pocket and pulled out a knife, similar to the one I'd taken from him during our scuffle by the Dumpster. He opened the blade and it locked in place with a click.

"Hold him tight, Earlly Whirlly."

"My arms are getting tired," Earl said.

"Shut up, fat boy. Don't be such a pussy."

Lester got on his knees at my feet and pulled my shoes and socks off. I tried to kick him in the face, but it was no use. He held my feet and sliced my soles lengthwise with the blade. I felt the pain of the cuts and the warmth of the blood and I turned my head to the side and tried to vomit but nothing came out.

Lester sat back down and lit another joint. One minute past eleven. I wondered what he was going to do to me next. I knew he was going to kill me, so I wished he would just get it over with. I thought about my first wife, Susan, and our daughter, Harmony, and I thought about Juliet and Brittney and how dear they were to me. Did I tell them enough? Did I show them? I couldn't bear the thought of life without them. If they were going to be vaporized along with hundreds of thousands of other people in LA, then it was just as well that I died today, too. And what kind of world would be left after a nuclear war anyway? Some sort of unfathomable postapocalyptic wasteland, I thought. The people unlucky enough to survive would be sick from radiation poisoning, and everyone would eventually starve to death because all the animals and crops would be poisoned, as well. It wasn't a world I wanted to be part of.

"Kill me," I said.

"What?"

"Take that blade and slide it across my throat and get it over with."

"Well that wouldn't be much fun now, would it?"

Earl was huffing and puffing. "Seriously, I'm getting tired," he said. "Can we go now?"

"Oh, we ain't done yet," Lester said. "We ain't done by a long shot. The party's just getting started."

"You ain't really gonna kill him, are you?"

"Why, of course I am. What the hell you think we came here for, you big fat dumb motherfucker."

"You calling me stupid?"

"Let's face it, Earlly Whirlly. You ain't the sharpest tool in the shed."

Earl got up, took a step toward Lester, and swung at him. Lester ducked and buried the knife blade in Earl's fat belly. He pulled it out and stabbed him again and again and again. Earl coughed and I could hear the gurgle in his throat and he coughed again and blood flew out and splattered on the Van Gogh print. The big man took one lumbering step toward the door and then fell forward like a tree.

Lester started toward me with the knife, but I had already reached into my pocket and pulled the .25 caliber pistol I'd bought from the drug dealer at the bus station. I aimed at his chest and squeezed the trigger and I kept squeezing it until all the bullets were gone.

My left hand was useless and I couldn't walk because of the cuts on my feet. I scooted to the wall where my phone had landed and I picked it up with my good hand and pressed the final digit to call Greg Sloan with my thumb. It was 11:21.

"This is Sloan."

"Greg, there's a bomb on the eighth floor of the Capitol tower, in Studio B. Actually it's two bombs. They're in the big Marshall speaker cabinets and they're set to go off at noon eastern."

"Who is this?"

"Nicholas Colt. You got to hurry. There's not much time left."

"Colt. Are you sure about the bombs?"

"Sure as shit. There's no time to explain. You got to move, man."

"I'll put in an evacuation order right away," he said. "We'll get everyone out of the building and block all the incoming traffic."

"You don't understand. These are nukes. Suitcase bombs. It's not going to do any good to evacuate everyone. It's a waste of time. You need to get someone in there to defuse those things."

"Jesus. All right, Colt. I'm on it."

We disconnected. I called nine-one-one and the dispatcher said someone had already called about the gunshots at the motel and that help was on the way.

The room looked like a horror show. There was blood everywhere. I scooted to the bed and managed to climb onto it and I pulled the pillowcases off the pillows and tied pressure bandages on my feet to stop the bleeding. I tightened the knots using my right hand and my teeth. It was a struggle, but I finally got it done. I was dizzy and thought I might be bleeding to death.

Eleven forty-two.

I punched in Juliet's number. Days later, I would learn that at approximately the same time she said *hello*, Jose Arias and Vincent Faza from the LAPD bomb squad, both former military Explosive Ordinance Disposal experts, entered Studio B on the eighth floor of the Capitol tower. They had brought a timer with an LED display so they would know exactly how much time they had. The timer said 17:39. Seventeen minutes and thirty-nine seconds until half of LA was blown to kingdom come.

"Hi, sweetheart," I said.

"You sound terrible. What's wrong?"

"A lot. A lot's wrong. Listen, I'm not going to be home when you get there, after all. You'll have to take a cab from the airport."

"Why won't you be there?"

"I'll be in the hospital in Nashville. If I'm still alive when the ambulance gets here."

"Oh my God. What happened?"

The Department of Energy had been notified, and they were on the way, but Arias and Faza knew they would never make it in time. Fuck waiting for the feds. They used a high-speed portable X-ray unit to scan the interiors of the Marshall cabinets, and right away they discovered a series of microswitches on the rear panels that would cause the devices to detonate if the panels were removed. If the panels were removed, half of LA would be blown to kingdom come. The timer now said 16:02.

"I got jumped by a couple of dishwashers," I said. "They're dead now, but they fucked me up good. I never should have come back to this motel."

"Are you bleeding?"

"Like a stuck pig. The son of a bitch named Lester cut the bottoms of my feet."

"You need to put pressure on the wounds so they'll clot."

"I wrapped my feet with pillowcases, but I couldn't get them tight enough. Lester also broke my left hand."

Her voice quivered up an octave. She was on the verge of crying. "Oh my God, Nicholas. I'm so sorry. My poor darling. If I were only there to help you. You said an ambulance is coming?"

Since the quickest and easiest access route was obviously out of the question, Arias and Faza took a few minutes to discuss alternatives. They knew from the X-rays that the systems contained collapsing circuits with relays held open by batteries. If the batteries were taken out, the relays would close and complete the circuit to the detonators and half of LA would be blown to kingdom come. They thought about shooting shaped charges through the power supplies, to cut off power from the detonators and render the devices inert. The shaped charges would have to beat the electricity to the detonator wires before the juice could get through. It was a tricky proposition, especially since they had to plan everything by X-ray. Placement had to be precise, and they doubted there was enough time.

"The ambulance should have been here by now," I said. "Jules, there's some things I need to talk to you about."

"I'm here. I'm not hanging up until I know you're safe."

"Do you know how much I love you?"

"I love you, too," she said.

Arias and Faza decided to try a hand entry. Very dangerous, but the only practical solution at this point. They donned night vision goggles and turned all the lights out in case the detonators were rigged with photocell relays. Faza cut the mesh grille on the front of the cabinets with a utility knife, and they each took a screwdriver and started working on removing the speakers.

"The good news," I said, "is that I didn't start smoking again. The bad news is I'm a drug addict now."

"What?"

"He turned me into a junkie, Jules."

"Who?"

"Brother John. It was the same Brother John who was at Chain of Light, only I didn't know it because his face was different. He got me hooked on Dilaudid. Now I'm slinking around bus stations and buying tar heroin from guys with gold teeth."

"We'll get you whatever help you need," she said. "Do you hear me, Nicholas? I love you no matter what."

Once the speakers were out of the way, Arias and Faza had twelve-inch holes to work through. Tight, but doable. Combination locks protected the cases surrounding the nuclear devices. Arias and Faza had predicted this, and there was a career criminal named Danny "Fingers" Gibson waiting in the wings. Arias called him in. The only other choice was to explosively open the cases, which would be quicker but might trigger the detonators and blow half of LA to kingdom come. Better to let Fingers give it a try, at least. Faza jammed a set of night vision goggles on his head and told him not to turn the lights on no matter what.

"No matter what?" I said.

"Yes. I'll love you no matter what. We'll get you into rehab, whatever it takes."

Fingers worked his magic, and the case surrounding the first device clicked open. From there it was a piece of cake. Faza carefully removed the mercury stem generator, a red cylinder the size of a cigarette that would initiate the nuclear reaction, and watched the adjoining capacitor bleed down on an amp meter. One down and one to go.

"My addiction isn't even the worst of it," I said. "I cheated on you, Jules. I was with another woman out in LA."

Silence.

Fingers ran into trouble with the second combination lock, and only one minute and twenty-four seconds remained on the timer. At that point, Arias and Faza decided to blow the second case open with a flexible, linear-shaped charge. They briefly entertained the notion of trying the waterjet disrupter, a sort of freestanding gun that resembled a two-foot praying mantis. It shot water with enough force to open metal containers, but they weren't a hundred percent sure it would work and with time this short they needed to be a hundred percent. The shaped charge was their only chance now. Faza wrapped one of the snakelike explosives around the case and taped a blasting cap to it while Arias and Fingers heaved the Steinway grand onto its side to use as a shield. All this took about half a minute. Faza then unreeled the wires connected to the blasting cap and joined the others behind the piano. He stared at the toggle switch on the firing device for a few seconds, hoping they had made the right decision. The electro-explosive would either safely open the case and give them access to the second mercury stem generator, or it would trigger the detonator to the nuclear device and half of LA would be blown to kingdom come. If half of LA were blown to kingdom come, it would in essence mean that the world would be blown to kingdom come.

"Jules?"

"I'm here."

"I wasn't myself at the time. I mean, literally. Brother John brainwashed me, and induced amnesia somehow. I thought my name was Alexander Maddox. I thought my friends called me Maddog, or just Dog. I swear to God, Jules, I would have never cheated on you if I'd known what I was doing."

More silence. I looked at the clock on the nightstand. 10:59, which was really 11:59. It ticked over to the top of the hour, and the phone went dead. I redialed Juliet's number, but the call went straight to voice mail.

CHAPTER FORTY-FOUR

Tiny tornados danced across the barren landscape, filling the air with dry sand the color of lead. The sand and the dark clouds overhead made everything look like a grainy black-and-white photograph, like an unimaginably horrific and grim movie.

One of my teachers in high school said that cockroaches are among the few species capable of surviving a nuclear holocaust. Apparently, he was right.

A year after the initial blast, I lay in a puddle of my own urine as the filthy six-legged motherfuckers crawled all over me. Gone were the pine trees and the live oaks and the flowers and the fish and deer. Gone were the jays and the hawks and the redbirds and the grass and the crops and even the weeds. Gone. Everything gone.

Except the cockroaches.

My body was covered with purplish blisters, some of which had popped and were oozing a sticky clear fluid, and some of the roaches were able to enter the open sores and burrow into my flesh. They crawled in and out of my ears and nostrils as well, and I was too weak to swat them away. I was too weak to move. One of them found the path to my brain and took a big bite, and that's when I woke up and started thrashing and shouting like a madman.

"Let me out of here! Turn me loose, goddamnit!"

I was disoriented, and for a minute I thought I was back at Brother John's compound. My arms and legs were strapped to the frame of a hospital bed. There was a bag of IV fluid hanging on a pole, and a heart monitor wailing an alarm with the number 177 flashing red on the display. Tubes and wires everywhere.

As horrible as my situation seemed at the moment, it wasn't nearly as horrible as my postapocalyptic nightmare. Thinking about it rattled my marbles back into place, and I remembered the last moments before I lost consciousness. I was talking to Juliet, and the phone went dead at precisely the time the bombs were supposed to explode.

While I wondered if my nightmare might be in the midst of coming true, a nurse ran in and fiddled with the heart monitor and told me I needed to calm down. I recognized her. It was Sharon, who had been taking care of Virgil Lamb.

"Am I at Nashville General?" I said.

"You are, and I have a bone to pick with you."

"Pick away. I'm not in much of a position to defend myself."

"You told me you were Virgil Lamb's son, but all your paperwork here says Nicholas Colt. You tricked me."

"Guilty as charged," I said. "Is that why you tied me to the bed?"

"You were combative, and we had to restrain you. I'll take the restraints off if you promise to be good."

"I promise."

She unbuckled the tethers and straightened my bed and piggybacked a small bag of fluid into the main line.

"What's that?" I said.

"It's an antibiotic. Your PICC line was infected. We had to take it out."

I looked at my left upper arm and sure enough, the PICC line was gone. My left hand was in a hard cast, nothing but the fingernails poking through, and my feet were wrapped with white gauze.

"Are you hungry?"

"I need something for pain."

"Where are you hurting?" she said.

"My hand. My feet. All over."

I felt nauseated and my body ached from head to toe. It felt like I had the flu.

"I think you have some morphine ordered. I'll check and see."

"I'm allergic to that," I said.

"You're allergic to morphine?"

"It gives me a rash. There's another one they always give me. Starts with a D, I think."

"Dilaudid?"

"That's it."

"I'll call the doctor and see. It might take a while to get the order and for pharmacy to get it in the computer. You want some Tylenol or Motrin in the meantime?"

"Motrin," I said.

She left and came back with the pill a few minutes later and a turkey croissant wrapped in cellophane and a carton of 2 percent milk. I swallowed the tablet with some milk and unwrapped the sandwich and took a couple of bites.

"I need to change the dressings on your feet," she said. "But I'll wait till I get the order for your pain medicine."

"OK."

"*If* I get it."

"What do you mean?"

"The doctor might not want to order Dilaudid. When you came in, they tested your urine for drugs of abuse, and you popped positive for cannabis and opiates."

"I took two hits on a joint with an old man in the woods when I was running for my life," I said. "And they gave me some morphine when I went to the ER for chest pain. That's all. Look at me. You trying to say I'm not really in pain?"

There was an intercom in the room, and a disembodied voice told Sharon that security was on the phone asking if it was OK if Mr. Colt had visitors.

"How many?" she said.

"Two. It's his wife and daughter."

Sharon looked at me. I nodded. I'd been granted a miracle, but all I could think about was getting a fix.

—m—

Juliet and Brittney stood at the doorway and gazed in timidly until Sharon waved them in. "I'll let y'all visit," she said. "Give me a call if you need anything."

"Thanks, Sharon," I said.

Brittney walked to the bed and gave me a hug and looked me over with teary eyes. "You sure can get yourself into some pickles," she said. "I'm so glad you're OK."

"I'm so glad you're OK too," I said. "I'm taking it California is still intact."

"What do you mean?"

"I figured it would have been on the news by now."

"What?"

I glanced at Juliet. She seemed to be deep in thought. She wouldn't make eye contact with me.

Two men, one in a gray suit and the other navy blue, darkened the doorway. Navy Blue was holding a briefcase. Gray Suit told Juliet and Brittney to please excuse them. He said they needed to talk to me in private and it would only take a few minutes.

"We'll be in the waiting area," Juliet said. She and Brittney left the room. Gray Suit closed the door.

"What's going on?" I said. "That was my family. I haven't seen them for a long time."

Navy Blue pulled out a trifold wallet and showed me a silver badge with the letters NEST stamped on the crest.

"Nuclear Emergency Support Team," he said. "Department of Energy. Have you told anyone about the situation at the Capitol building in Los Angeles?"

"Not that I know of," I said. "The nurse told me I was combative. They had to restrain me. I don't remember any of that. I guess I could have said a lot of things while I was in that state."

"We'll check it out. But to your knowledge, you haven't told anybody?"

"Correct."

"We have some papers you need to sign."

"What papers?"

"It's imperative that you never, as long as you live, utter a word of your knowledge of the nuclear event in Los Angeles to another living soul."

"The bombs exploded?"

"No. The Los Angeles Police Department's bomb squad got there in time, but it's still what we call an event. It was a close call." He told me about Arias and Faza and the safecracker named Fingers.

"Knowledge of such an event could cause widespread panic," Gray Suit said. "One of our jobs is to prevent that. You're going to be tempted at some point to tell a friend, or your wife, or someone else who doesn't have the need to know. You're going to be tempted to sell the story to a publisher for seven figures. Don't do it."

"And what happens if I do tell someone?" I said.

"You don't want to know."

Navy Blue snapped open the briefcase and handed me a clipboard with a single sheet of paper on it.

"I need my glasses," I said.

"Is that them?" He pointed to the bedside table.

I put the reading glasses on and read the short contract. *As a matter of national security, blah, blah, blah.* He handed me a pen and I signed the paper.

"Thank you for your cooperation, Mr. Colt. Hopefully, this will be our first and last meeting. Here's one of our business cards. Keep it in a safe place. If anyone besides a United States agent tries to communicate with you regarding this matter, or if you need to talk to us for any reason, call the number on the card. We're available twenty-four-seven."

He shut the briefcase and Gray Suit followed him out the door. I'd dealt with government agents before, but these two were the strangest ever. It was as if any semblance of personality had been completely erased. I wondered if they had been to one too many nuclear test sites.

A couple of minutes later, Juliet came in alone.

"Where's Brittney?" I said.

"I sent her downstairs to get a soda. I figured we could use a few minutes to ourselves."

"OK."

"When you told me you had been with another woman, my initial reaction was anger. To me, that is the ultimate betrayal. Unforgivable. That's why I hung up on you, and why I wouldn't answer when you called back."

"I understand," I said. "But like I told you, I wasn't myself at the time."

"I'm still trying to wrap my head around that," she said. "I find it hard to believe that you—"

"Don't you trust me, Jules? I didn't have to tell you about it at all."

"So why did you? Are you in love with her?"

"Of course not. It meant nothing. I wasn't myself, and it meant nothing. I told you because I thought I was on my deathbed. It was a dying man's confession. I didn't think I would ever see you again."

"But you're here, and I'm here, and now we have to deal with it."

"We need to put it behind us," I said.

Brittney walked in with two cans of Pepsi and a Mountain Dew. She set all three on the bedside table and popped the tops and handed me the Dew. She knew it was my favorite.

"Thanks," I said. I took a sip and looked at my broken hand. "Hell, I guess I won't be able to open my own soda for a while. I guess I won't be able to do a lot of things for a while."

"That's what we're here for," Brittney said. She smiled and looked at me with those big blue eyes and my heart melted and I knew everything was going to be all right.

I pushed the call button and asked Sharon if she'd gotten the order for the Dilaudid yet.

CHAPTER FORTY-FIVE

For the first time in my life, I remembered what The Potato Man had told me in my dream. *The writing's on the wall*, he'd said.

Only the wall he was talking about was spelled W-A-H-L.

For whatever reason, Donna had purposely shoved me head-first into an intricate maze of unimaginable horrors. I was almost sure of it. Maybe Derek and Brother John had threatened her. Maybe she thought betraying me was the only way to save herself. Or maybe I would never know her true motivation. Maybe she would take the secret to her grave. Maybe, but I was counting on that not being the case.

Six weeks after I left Nashville General, I drove to Gainesville and climbed the steps to her front porch and rang the doorbell. The .38 I call Little Bill was holstered on my right hip, hidden by the tails of my Hawaiian shirt. Donna answered the door with a plastic cup in her hand filled with ice and a clear liquid.

"Nicholas. What are you doing here?"

"Just wanted to talk to you for a minute," I said.

"I'm really kind of busy. Maybe we could—"

"You're not busy. That's vodka in your cup, and I can hear the TV blaring. I need to talk to you about what happened at the Capitol Records building. Can I come in?"

She frowned and stepped aside. I walked into the foyer. I followed her to the living room and sat beside her on the faux suede sofa. She grabbed the remote and muted the television.

"What's with the brace?" she said. She gestured toward my left hand.

"I had a little accident in Tennessee. Have the feds been to see you?"

"What?"

"The federal agents."

"I don't know what you're talking about."

"I think you do know. But if they haven't been to see you, then they don't know you know. You know?"

"Nicholas—"

"Let me tell you something, Donna. I might not be able to prove it in court, but I know you were involved in all this. Somehow, you were involved. Everything was too much of a coincidence for you not to be. The murders at the Lambs' residence on Thanksgiving Day. Your brother, Derek, being the only officer on duty and responding to the nine-one-one call. Brother John being the same Brother John I'd tangled with at Chain of Light three years ago. The tilted crucifixes. That was the kicker, wasn't it? You knew about the Leitha Ryan case here in Florida, and you knew those forehead crosscuts would draw me in. But why, why in *hell* would a stealthy neo-Nazi group like the Harvest Angels want to draw attention to itself by using a calling card like that? That's what I should have asked myself in the first place. That's where I fucked up royally. I should have known it was a setup from the get-go. There were no other instances of murders with that MO other than Leitha Ryan. That was all for me, wasn't it?"

She set her drink on the glass-and-chrome table beside the couch. Her eyes were bloodshot from the alcohol.

"What do you want me to do?" she said. "Give you a nice tidy confession like they do in the movies? Get the fuck out of my house."

"I know you were involved, and I'm going to do everything I can to see that you're punished for it." I glanced at her laptop on the coffee table, and then back to her. "It's all going to make a very interesting book, isn't it? How much have you told your agent already?"

She swallowed hard. "Get the fuck out of my house," she said again.

So I did. I got the fuck out of her house.

Before I left the driveway, I called the number on the card Navy Blue had given me.

CHAPTER FORTY-SIX

Six months and three surgeries after I drove away from Donna Wahl's house, I sat in the waiting room of a methadone clinic in Jacksonville feeling sorry for myself. My hand worked well enough to screw the top off a jar of peanut butter, but it didn't work well enough to play the guitar and it never would. I tried to tell myself I was lucky to be alive, and that in time I would learn to live with the loss and fill the void somehow, but something dear had been taken from me and I couldn't help feeling a certain amount of rage every time I thought about it.

I couldn't make money as a musician anymore, and my PI license had been suspended indefinitely pending some criminal charges I faced in Tennessee. I'd been cleared in the deaths of Lester and Earl, but the police had impounded my Ford Focus rental car and had found the two packets of black tar heroin and my slam kit. My attorney said I would get off with probation, no problem, but it was doubtful that I would ever be able to work as a private investigator again. Not legally, anyway.

My professional life was totally fucked up, and my private life wasn't much better. Juliet and I were in counseling, but she wasn't ready to stay in the same house with me yet. I was back living in the Airstream at Joe's Fish Camp.

"Hey, you got a cigarette?"

The girl sitting three seats to my right in the methadone clinic waiting room had long blonde hair and blue eyes. She reminded me of Brittney, only way thinner. Brittney had gotten accepted to the University of Florida. She was in the middle of her first semester, living in one of the freshman dorms with a roommate named Cai. Cai was from China. Brittney helped Cai with English, and Cai helped Brittney with calculus. I was proud of my girl, and I told her so every chance I got.

"I don't smoke," I said. "I quit a long time ago."

"Got a dollar I can borrow? I need to get some diapers for my baby."

"Where's your baby?"

"At home with his daddy."

I pulled out my wallet and handed her a five. I knew it would probably go for a pack of smokes and a pint of beer, but I didn't care. I knew there was no baby.

"Wow. Thanks. You know, I was just thinking. You don't look like you belong here."

"Funny," I said. "I was just thinking the same thing."

"I mean, you just don't see many junkies your age. No offense or anything, but most hypes either kick young or die young."

"None of them die young," I said. "Only the good die young."

"Hey, isn't that a song?"

"Yeah."

The girl at the clinic seemed interested in me for some reason. Maybe I was the only person who had ever given her five bucks without expecting something in return.

"What kind of work do you do?" she said.

"I'm a private investigator," I said, just to be saying something. I didn't want to admit I was a bum. "Insurance fraud, cheating spouses, deadbeat dads. Stuff like that."

"Sounds boring."

"It is."

"Is this your first time here?" she said.

"How did you know?"

"Just never seen you around before. You going to do group and all?"

The thought of sitting in a circle trading stories with a bunch of strung-out hypes made my stomach churn.

"I'll do whatever it takes," I said.

"So how did you quit smoking? God, I think that's even harder than smack. I mean, you don't get dope-sick or anything, but it's still hard as shit."

The lady at the counter called my name. I told the girl I'd see her later.

On the way to the counter, I thought about the last question she asked me, about how I quit smoking. *It's easy to quit smoking. I've done it a thousand times*, Mark Twain once said. And it was true. I had quit a bunch of times myself. I had used nicotine patches and lozenges and gum, and drugs like Zyban and Chantix. I had tried hypnosis, and I had read every book published on the subject, but the last time I quit, the time that had stuck, I didn't do any of that. The last time I quit, I went cold turkey. The last time I quit, I walked by a trash can and threw away half a pack and resolved to never buy another as long as I lived. It was the hardest thing I'd ever done, and four years after the fact I was still dreaming about the damn things sometimes. Once an addict, always an addict. It never leaves you. It's like getting bitten by a vampire. It's forever. What you have to do is recognize it for what it is, and then learn to live with it. You can never really defeat it. You can only keep it at bay.

The lady at the counter handed me a pill bottle with my name and social security number on it, and a paper cup half full of water. There was no lid on the pill bottle. It had one pill in it, a small round white tablet. I looked at it and rattled it around in the bottom of the bottle. I was supposed to swallow it while the lady watched. I handed the bottle back to her.

"This is not for me," I said. I turned and walked away. I didn't look at the girl I'd given the five dollars to on my way out. I kept my eyes on the exit door.

I drove back to my campsite at Lake Barkley. When I opened the door to get out of my '96 GMC Jimmy, the sandy-haired dog we call Bud came running up wagging his tail. He had his piece of nylon rope in his mouth. He wanted to play tug-of-war.

"I'm not in the mood, Bud," I said.

He dropped the rope and barked at me playfully. When I started inside, he nipped at my heels.

"You're a persistent motherfucker, you know that? Kind of like me, I guess."

I played tug-of-war with him for a few minutes and then gave him a nice long back scratch and belly rub. I opened the door to the Airstream and let him inside and gave him a Milk Bone. I had one foil packet of black tar heroin in the little cupboard over the sink. One more time, I thought, and that would be it. I sat down at the table with my kit and started to unwrap the foil. Bud sat on the floor and looked up at me curiously.

"I know what you're thinking," I said. "One more time's not going to be enough. It's never enough. I'll slam this one, and then I'll hustle up enough money to get some more. Right?"

He started panting. I took it as a yes.

I got up and walked outside and tossed the packet into the rusty drum I use for burning trash. Bud had followed me out, and he had the piece of rope in his mouth again.

"I gotta go, Bud."

I wanted to talk to Juliet before I started getting sick. I wanted to tell her how much I loved her, and how much I wanted things to be right between us again.

I opened the door and started to climb into the Jimmy. Bud dropped the rope and wagged his tail, obviously hoping I might let him tag along.

"Maybe next time," I said, scratching his ears. Then I thought what the hell. I opened the passenger's side door and he jumped in and we drove away.

THE END

ABOUT THE AUTHOR

Jude Hardin holds a Bachelor of Arts degree in English from the University of Louisville. His debut thriller, *Pocket-47*, recently received a starred review in *Publisher's Weekly*. Hardin is also one of the authors for the Dead Man series of horror thrillers created by Lee Goldberg and William Rabkin. When not pounding away at the computer keyboard, Hardin can be found at home in north Florida pounding on his drums, playing tennis, reading, or fishing in the pond with his son.